War Stories

War Stories

Elisabeth Doyle

Two Harbors Press

Copyright © 2012 by Elisabeth Doyle.

Two Harbors Press
212 3rd Avenue North, Suite 290
Minneapolis, MN 55401
612.455.2293
www.TwoHarborsPress.com

All rights reserved. No part of this publication may be reproduced, stored in a retrieval system, or transmitted, in any form or by any means, electronic, mechanical, photocopying, recording, or otherwise, without the prior written permission of the author.

This is a work of fiction. Names, places, and incidents are the products of the author's imagination or are used fictitiously. The characters depicted are not intended to represent actual persons, living or dead.

ISBN-13: 978-1-937928-40-7
LCCN: 2012932732

Cover by 48th Avenue Productions
Cover photographs by Elisabeth Doyle, with thanks to M. Sandoval, R. Meteer, and O. Chase

Distributed by Itasca Books

Printed in the United States of America

*To my loved ones, who always believed that
this book was possible.*

Contents

Recruiters	1
One Of These Days It Will All Be Over	13
Pistolesi	23
Driving	41
The Deepest, Darkest Part of the Woods	51
Graduation	67
Median	75
Love Spell	87
Passengers	100

Recruiters

The gas station was quiet that night – the gas station where Manny worked. Right on the strip, bordered by a liquor store on one side and a Chinese take-out on the other. At the take-out, a woman took orders through a thick sheet of bulletproof plastic and slid the food out through a narrow slot above the counter. It was the same at the gas station - the attendant sat behind a dense wall of Plexiglas, punctured with small holes that allowed for the passage of sound. The wall had gone up the year before, after Manny's father was shot and killed by a junkie while he worked the cash register. When they found him the next morning the floor was covered with large, burgundy blossoms and there was blood on the walls and on the candy and chewing gum.

The police came by and took some pictures and said things like "We'll be in touch." After that, Manny put up the plastic barrier.

But that was a long time ago, last summer, already. Now Manny and his mother minded the store and the pumps alone.

On that particular night, it was hot, mid-July, and the sound of the highway was muted in the background. Manny's mother dozed behind the cash register and Manny sat out on the curb with a Pepsi in his hand. He watched as the cars passed by on the boulevard, slowing occasionally to engage the prostitutes who stood like human targets in the shadow of the overpass. Manny felt frightened for the women as they approached the vehicles, fragile and defiant and with nothing in the world to protect them.

After awhile a girl and a boy pulled into the station, kids Manny knew from school. They were driving around in a pick-up truck that the boy had just bought, second or third-hand. They filled up the tank and asked Manny to go riding with them. Manny knew the boy, Ernie, from the neighborhood – everyone knew him because his brother had been killed in Vietnam the summer before, the first of several on the block. Now Ernie was planning to go, too.

"If it was good enough for Wop, it's good enough for me," he'd say.

Ernie's brother was called Wop. Wop was a big boy, with muscles around his neck and veins that stood out in his forearms. He'd been in jail a couple of times, not for anything too bad. The first time it was for breaking into a pharmacy, and the other time it was because he'd shoplifted a clock radio.

Wop worked on cars and he was good with them. He did tune-ups from out of his driveway, and that's how the recruiters found him. They cruised up and down the neighborhood streets in an unmarked gray Ford, stopping boys wherever they could. They stopped boys in the parking lots, in shopping malls, in the bowling alley, and on the street corners. They didn't care if the boys were skinny or fat or short or tall. But their gray, nondescript car had broken down one day when they were out looking for boys, and they found themselves in Wop's driveway, with Wop toiling under the hood for them. They liked Wop right off, because he looked big and strong. He looked like he could carry an M-60 machine gun on his back as well as about 100 pounds of other stuff. And that's exactly what he did when he joined the war, until he stepped on some kind of a booby trap and it blew him way up in the air, and when he came back down he didn't even look like Wop anymore.

"They coulda put a monkey carcass in that box and we wouldn't have known the difference," Ernie said, after the funeral.

After Wop died, Ernie and Manny would stare at the military dress photo that sat on the top of the television, awestruck. The deadpan stare. The short hair.

"He was so different, man," Ernie would say. "We went to the graduation and he was like a different guy. All formal with us and shit, like we were people he was just meeting for the first time or something."

The recruiters caught up with Ernie, too, as soon as he turned seventeen. They pulled up alongside him like ghosts in their gray car.

"It was like they just appeared, man. I didn't even hear them coming," Ernie said.

They showed him pictures, he said. They made him promises. It was like a man wooing a foreign bride. They also said something about picking up where Wop left off, not letting Wop's death be in vain – something like that, and Ernie bought it. But it was more than that, too. It wasn't just the recruiters, you couldn't blame it all on them. It was the photo. It was Wop changing, being changed.

"There ain't nothing around here that's going to change me," Ernie said. "Wop was like a different person. I wanna be someone different, too."

So that night, to celebrate Ernie's departure for boot camp, Manny waved goodbye to his mother and got into the truck. Ernie stopped at the liquor store and then they went four-wheeling under the bridge, near the refineries, in a toxic-smelling area of swamp. The girl, whose name was Marisol, sat on Manny's lap. Manny knew Marisol from school, but just a little bit. Enough to have heard the chatter; that her mother's boyfriend had taken her and her sisters to a nude beach and taken movies of them, certain kinds of movies, and sold them. Marisol didn't talk much. There was something about her that made Manny's heart hurt.

Anyway, that night, Marisol sat on his lap as they four-wheeled, screaming at the top of their lungs as Ernie went full-speed through the ditches and muck. Marisol's long, blue-black hair flew into his mouth, scratchy like paint bristles, and they bounced to the top of the cab and hit their heads, hard. It was crazy, Ernie's driving, because he'd only just gotten his license, and barely.

Later on they stopped at a party, they didn't know who the house belonged to but there were kids everywhere, drinking from kegs, playing quarter-bounce, making out in the bedrooms. They stayed in the kitchen and drank beers, and put some music on, and when they were all a little bit tipsy they huddled together in the middle of the kitchen and slow-danced, the three of them. Manny could feel Marisol's arm around his waist and could smell the scent of whatever detergent she used, it smelled like no soap he had ever smelled before, sweet and spicy.

Afterwards, on the way back to the gas station, Marisol leaned back and put her arm around Manny's shoulders, and he felt something coming open and bubbling up inside himself. He wanted to fall asleep like that, holding her that way forever, but then Ernie was driving too fast and gunned it through a red light, and a milk truck sped into the intersection in front of them. Ernie's mouth made a big "O" and Manny said the F-word, really soft almost, and his hands went out to the dashboard. Marisol didn't see anything, although she may have felt Manny's shoulders stiffen and clench as she leaned against him, her eyes closed, feeling a peace and safety that she'd never felt in her whole life before, not ever. So she didn't see it – didn't even know what was happening as the pick-up slammed into the side of the milk truck and her body kept on traveling through space, at just the same speed that they'd been driving – 75. She left the crumpling vehicle behind, propelled through the shattering windshield and out into the darkness.

The driver of the milk truck was thrown from his vehicle and into the parking lot of the Salvation Army ministry. Ernie was dead, his body half draped over the front of the pick-up, facing upward. He had on a T-shirt that said "have a nice day," with two eyes and a smile underneath. Manny was only partially conscious but he could see his friend, and he wondered how Ernie had gotten turned around like that, facing the sky, and why his face wasn't inside the engine. Ernie's eyes were open wide and he had a slight smile on his lips, as if someone had just surprised him with something pleasant. Marisol was on her way into the atmosphere, her body wrapped around a telephone pole, her spirit becoming whole again and engulfed in light. Manny, who'd been shielded by the weight of Marisol, had cuts on his head and hands and a broken arm and broken rib.

A young police officer was the first one on the scene. After surveying the wreck he unraveled the yellow tape, gently, and cordoned off the area around the accident. It was his first night ever on patrol, and he waited a few minutes before he called for back-up and the EMTs. He felt like he had come across something special and sacred and intimate, that he was very fortunate to have encountered such a scene on his first night out. He felt like a gift was being given him and he wanted to hold onto it. There was no urgency; the silence of the scene and his cursory investigation told him that most of these people were either dead or dying.

The young officer looked down at Ernie, who smiled up at him. He went over to Marisol, her limbs bent in all directions, in ways he had never imagined. One arm reached awkwardly across her body like it wasn't attached to her, like it was someone else's arm. She lay on her side, hugging the base of the telephone pole and staring at the blacktop. The officer tried to imagine the girl as she was just a few minutes before, when she was living. Her open eyes seemed kind and intelligent.

The night around them was very still, and there was no sound except for Manny's gentle, intermittent moans. In the absence of a priest, the young officer felt it was his role to mediate between this world and the next for these unfortunate people he had found. He wanted to do so before the back-up cars arrived and the dignity of the scene was disturbed forever. So he closed his eyes and tried to imagine them, rising out of their bodies and drifting far above the crushed cars on the boulevard, above all the grief and loneliness, and he asked God to help them on their journey.

When back-up arrived, more officers littered the scene and began getting busy. One of them, another new guy, hung back. The young officer, the one who did the benediction, said to him - "It's beautiful, isn't it?"

The ambulances came after awhile, and they wrapped Ernie and Marisol and the milk truck driver in blue plastic tarps, and put Manny on a stretcher. In the meantime, the recruiters drove by in their ghost car. They got out and looked around them, and they recognized Ernie.

"Shit, that's one of our recruits," one of them said.

"This place is a shit-hole," the other one said. "You can't keep them alive long enough to go over and get killed."

The men chortled to one another at this, and then they drove away again with the radio turned on.

In the hospital, they gave Manny a cast and sewed up the cuts on his head. Then they looked in his eyes with a light and told him that he had a concussion, and shouldn't let himself fall asleep for 24 hours. When the nurse wheeled him out of the ER they passed a little room, a cubicle, where a body lay. There was a curtain that could have been closed, but it wasn't. A pale blue sheet was pulled all the way up over the person's head and a sneaker stuck out from underneath.

Before they released him, the nurse gave Manny a bottle of painkillers in case his arm started hurting, or his ribs. She told him that he couldn't stay at the hospital because other people were coming in who needed help worse than he did, knife wounds and gun shots and that kind of thing. Then she wheeled him to the back exit and asked if he could walk. His cuts were bleeding through the gauze and his arm was strapped to his side in a sling.

"I guess so," Manny said.

When Manny returned to the gas station, his mother screamed.

"What happened to you?" She yelled. Her voice was panicked and desperate.

Manny felt confused, like he wasn't sure what had happened, really. He wanted to tell her something, but he couldn't, he couldn't seem to make his words or thoughts line up in a sentence.

"There was a girl in my lap," was all he could say.

Later that evening, Manny minded the station while his mother slept on a cot in the back of the store. His head ached and his arm hurt, and his thoughts felt upside-down and confused. It was like nothing had happened, like he had dreamt it; but he knew that something had happened, because he felt a dark, hollow feeling starting to seep into him, brought on by the proximity to death.

At about 3 a.m., two girls came into the station, on foot. They had a baby with them. Manny was asleep on the pavement outside the store, he had forgotten about the 24 hour thing because his head wasn't working right. The girls didn't want any gas. They bickered about what to buy – milk, diapers, cigarettes, a bag of Chee-tos. They counted out their money in coins. They were plain girls, not like Marisol –

Marisol the mysterious, the ethereal. Their hair was unwashed and pulled harshly away from their faces, and their teeth and skin were bad. One of them had track marks creeping up the inside of her arm. The baby watched them, its brow furrowed, pondering its fate and future at the hands of these two people, and wondering why it had been born into this particular set of circumstances while other babies were born into other circumstances.

Manny woke up and took their coins, which amounted to less than one-half of the bill, and put the items in a plastic bag. The painkillers made him feel like he was moving in slow motion, like he was watching himself from someplace very far away.

After awhile, the girls left the store with their groceries. Manny watched them for as long as he could, until they melted into the darkness beyond the illumination of the pump island. As they stepped onto the littered sidewalk that bordered the highway, some boys pulled up alongside them, howling. One of them leaned out the car window and made an obscene gesture with his hands. The girls gave him the "F-you" sign and kept on walking.

From several doors down, in the parking lot of the 7-11, the recruiters watched. The front seat of their vehicle was littered with Tasty-Kake wrappers and soda cans and donut boxes. They watched as Manny sat down on the pavement outside the gas station and started retching. He looked like a mummy with all the bandages over his head and blood coming through. He looked like a lost cause, like a lonely lost soul, with no one keeping watch over him. The recruiters thought about this and then they looked at one another and smiled.

Then they pulled their vehicle out onto the boulevard, past the prostitutes who stood in the shadow of the overpass, past the weary glow of the liquor store and the Chinese take-out.

Manny caught sight of the grey car as it pulled into the gas station. From where he sat, leaning against one of the gas pumps, he held up his middle finger. The recruiters laughed. It didn't matter. It was only a matter of time before the boy realized the power of the particular currency they offered.

Manny's head was starting to swim and spin with the painkillers now. All the recruiters had to do was keep up.

One Of These Days
It Will All Be Over

It was a warm morning and Diego was on his way to the South Side to pick up his children, his little boy and girl. He took them to school on Tuesdays and Thursdays, so that his wife, who worked the late shift, could sleep in. His wife's name was Marlene. When Diego was in the army, in boot camp and then overseas, he'd carried her letters in the liner of his helmet or inside his shirt, until the sweat made the ink bleed and run and fade. He looked at her photograph in the morning and the evening, until it became crepey and withered.

Marlene was pregnant when he left for the war. She gave birth to their first child, Jenny, six months into his tour. The next day, Diego went to a jewelry shop in Cholon, the teeming, impenetrable Chinatown on the far side of Saigon, and had his lighter engraved. On one side it said "Jenny." On the other side, it said "One of these days it will all be over."

By the time Jenny was born, Diego had seen and done a lot of things. His best friend, Felix, had stepped on a mine that was covered with some leaves and twigs. He wasn't paying attention, so he stepped on the mine and it shot him straight up into the air. When he came down he had no legs, the legs were someplace else entirely. Diego held Felix while the medic shot him up with morphine, again and again, and then it was over. Once you give someone that much morphine, Diego knew, they let go. A wounded body won't hold on without the effort of the mind. It's like it takes concentration to stay alive, Diego thought.

But Felix was only one side of things. Diego had to take life, too. After many months, he had taken more lives than he could count, he had witnessed and engaged in cruelties of which he had not imagined himself capable. When he returned home, he felt ugly and maimed inside. He felt like a stranger in his own house.

"I'm not the same man," he told his wife. "I'm nothing now."

She put her arms around him. "I know you're not the same man," she said. "You're different now. Everyone changes. You've been changed."

Diego shook his head. Sometimes he would lie in bed and weep, and think about the things he'd done and what his life had come to.

"How can God love me?" He would cry.

After a few months at home, Diego started drinking. He didn't work. He spent the day down at the basketball court on the corner, playing pick-up games. He'd walk all around the city and ride the trains – all the way uptown, then all the way downtown, to Howard, to 95th. He wandered around the city with no place to go, staring at his reflection in the glass storefronts. His hair was growing wild and outward and his cheeks were rough with stubble. In some ways, he looked like other boys his age, but he was not like those boys anymore.

After awhile, Marlene got pregnant again and she begged Diego to look for a job. There was no money, and they argued. After he'd raised his hand to her more than once, and pawned their stereo and wedding rings, she put him out. Then Diego went to live in a rooming house and took a job as a janitor, and he kept on drinking.

On that morning, Diego did what he always did on Tuesdays and Thursdays; he picked up his children from his wife's place on the South Side. They were wearing matching plaid coats with blue buttons, and blue berets. They carried matching blue lunchboxes. When Diego saw them, he felt his heart pound and his eyes filled up with tenderness. The children smiled at him, but there was something in their expression that was fearful and pulled back, even now, after several years.

That morning, the children clung to their mother until she announced that it was time to go, and then they approached Diego gingerly and took his hands. Then they left the apartment.

The subway platform was already crowded when they arrived. There were men with briefcases and long coats, and women wearing colorful dresses and make-up. Diego watched them pass. He wondered where they were going, what kinds of jobs they had. They all looked happy and successful, like they had someplace important to go. Here and there, groups of teenagers crowded together in clusters, laughing and flirting.

Diego stood stiffly on the platform, his charges on either side of him. He didn't really know how to talk with children, and they seemed just as content to stay silent. Every once in a while they would look up at him with soulful, watchful eyes, and Diego would smile down at them. He tried to arrange his expression in a way that seemed happy and confident, although that was not at all the way he felt inside.

As they waited for the train, Diego continued his inventory of the crowd around them. Some boys in school uniforms dribbled a basketball. A couple nuzzled on one of the benches, and when they kissed, Diego looked away. He didn't like to see that. Further down the platform, a young man in a knee-length raincoat stood next to the tracks, reading a newspaper. His hair was neatly parted on the side and his shoes were shined. He wore a white shirt, open at the collar. Diego stared down at his own shoes – scuffed brown work boots, worn all the way down at the heel.

Diego and his children stood there on the platform for several minutes, not speaking, until they heard a loud grunt and turned together to where the young man had been standing, reading the newspaper. The boy wasn't reading anymore - he had slipped and was lying on his side on the cement. At first Diego thought it was a joke. Other people thought the same and they moved away from the boy, disapproving. When the boy started to get to his feet the people seemed relieved, and they turned back to whatever they'd been doing.

As the minutes passed, the people began to grow impatient, and they looked down the track and at their watches. Diego, too, began to stare into the tunnel, until a woman's shout pierced the silence of the subway station. When he turned, Diego saw people running to the side of the tracks, to the part of the platform where the young man had been standing. They were hovering and looking down onto the rails like they were looking into a wishing well.

Diego moved toward the edge of the platform, his children in tow. He pushed some people aside and peered down at what they were watching – the young man, thrashing and kicking, his eyes rolled back and the tendons in his neck bulging.

"It's a seizure!" someone yelled.

Diego stared at the boy, along with everyone else, until he heard a rumbling, and some shouts, and a number of people in the crowd began pointing down the track at a small pinpoint of light.

Diego looked at the boy convulsing below, and then he jumped down onto the track. He didn't remember jumping down, he was just suddenly there. It surprised him as much as anyone, as if he had suddenly materialized on the railroad ties like a ghost. Diego lay down against the boy and tried to gather him over his shoulders, the way he had in the army with a wounded buddy, or a dead buddy, their bodies heavy like sacks of cement mix. But this boy was stiff and contorting, fighting him, and Diego's own body had wasted and atrophied in the years since the war. Down the track, a faint glow had begun to spread.

"Look!" Some people cried, pointing. "Look!"

Diego wished that some of the other people would come onto the track and help him, but they didn't. The light in the tunnel was unmistakable now, not just a glow, but a distinct sphere of light moving toward them. The children screamed in unison. Other people were screaming, too. Diego could hear the hum of the train and the vibrations of the rails. It would not be possible to lift the boy from the track now.

Diego's children were at fever pitch now, wailing. People were shouting – "Get out of there, man, get out! It can't be helped!" But Diego didn't get out. Instead, he heaved the boy's body into the small space between the rail and the wall, and pressed his own body against the boy's, forcing him to be still. The boy's face was against Diego's jaw, and Diego could hear the strange, gravelly gnashing of teeth. They were like a mirror image of one another – face to face, hands against hands, torso against torso. Every inch of Diego pressed into the boy, willing him flat. He squeezed his eyes closed and held his breath as the train descended. He could feel the rush of air along his backbone and brushing against the back of his cap. The vibrations made his teeth rattle and the sound consumed him.

The people on the platform watched in horror as the train rushed by.

"My God!" someone cried. The screams of the children combined with the screech of the train as it passed.

Then it was over. The train howled down the track and out of sight. The people hid their faces. They couldn't bear to look, but they needed to look. They fought with themselves about it, some of them peeking through their fingers. But where they expected to see gore and mangled flesh on the track, there was none. There was only Diego, and the boy, pressed against the track wall, utterly still.

After awhile, the ambulance came for the boy, whose seizure had passed and who was now sitting up and talking to the police officers. They shooed everyone back behind a yellow line, and the people resented it. They were like clumsy intruders, the police, treading oblivious on hallowed ground.

"Why are you shooing us back?" the people said to the officers. "We were the ones who were here, not you. We bore witness to this. You have no right to separate us from what belongs to us. Let us be."

Eventually the people began to ascend the subway steps back into the daylight. Their minds felt fuzzy and far away. They didn't speak much – not to each other, not to the people around them. They went to their jobs, most of them, but sat at their desks and could not work.

The police asked Diego some questions in disbelief, not quite knowing what to ask but feeling they should ask him something, feeling that the incident warranted a report of some kind. When they finished, Diego and his children were left alone on the platform, while the police un-did the yellow tape and talked to someone on the radio about routing trains through the station again. Diego's children clutched his hands, one on either side, and eventually they, too, ascended the stairs back into the morning.

The children didn't go to school that day, and Diego didn't go to work. They went to a nearby park, and sat on a small bench under a dogwood tree. They didn't say anything. Some boys played basketball in the distance. A young woman slept on a park bench, a filthy sleeping bag bunched around her. The children huddled against Diego on either side, clutching him. He kept both of his arms around their shoulders, and they watched as the day passed. The sun rose high above them and crested there, diminishing all shadow, and then began its slow descent.

When the afternoon grew cold, and the shadows fell across the trees and the sun no longer fixed its light upon them, they got up.

Pistolesi

She took the job after Ronnie got home. The benefit check was small and they could barely make the rent. Ronnie didn't want to look for work.

"Who's going to hire me?" He said.

Ronnie had lost one eye and the right side of his head had shrapnel in it, and he had to learn how to do certain things again, like for the first time. He had to learn how to tie his shoes again, and to say words like "bathrobe." When they sent him home from the VA, they told him they'd arrange for a therapist to come out to the house to work with him, but no one came. They lived on an unpaved road up in the hills around Harmon, so Eveline figured that maybe the therapist just couldn't find them, or maybe they didn't have therapists like that out there.

Ronnie didn't talk much when he came home. Mostly, he just watched television in the basement or went on the computer. He lost his temper and screamed at her sometimes, and sometimes he hit out. One time he twisted her arm so badly that it did something to her shoulder, and another time he pushed her into a bookcase.

Sometimes Eveline would watch Ronnie, struggling and angry and with his terrible wound, and she'd try to remember him as he had been. She remembered when he was in basic training, how they weren't allowed to see family until the very last day, until graduation. It was right after high school, after they'd been married in the fall and she got pregnant in the spring. In the beginning he would sneak out and call her every few days, from a 7-11 near the base. Sometimes he wouldn't say anything, he would just cry. But after awhile the calls became less frequent, and then they stopped altogether. In those months, Eveline knew that something was happening to her husband, that he was being changed. He was learning to keep himself apart from her, in some part of his mind and spirit, and she knew that he would never belong to her in the same way again.

Now they had a baby, Ginger, and Ronnie didn't even want to hold her. He barely even looked at her.

"I'm not the same," Ronnie said.

"I know you're not," Eveline said. "You're different now. You've been through something. Everybody changes."

Secretly, inside herself, she wanted to be changed, too, or at least she thought she did. Wanting to be changed, she would ask him, again and again, "What was it like?"

But Ronnie could never tell her what it was like, and that was the sign of a true adventure, she thought; it changes you in some way that you can't articulate, you can't convey. It stays hidden inside you forever.

After awhile, Ronnie started going into town and getting

tattoos – big, black blobs and strange symbols all over his body. Eventually they covered his chest and arms. Eveline went snooping on the computer and found some photographs that Ronnie's friends had sent him, from the war. Some of them she couldn't make out, they were images that made no sense to her. A sheet. A bag. A foot. A limp pile of rags. Here and there, there were photos of a small figure shrouded in black, a woman or a girl, surrounded by men in military uniforms. Eveline called the VA again.

"Can you send that therapist?" she asked.

After several months the landlord sent them an eviction notice, and Eveline decided to look for work. When she read the classifieds, though, she saw that there was nothing out there that she wanted to do, and nothing she was qualified to do, either. They made her feel tired and hopeless and like all there was in life was being a bartender or a telemarketer, or maybe a cocktail waitress. Finally she answered an ad in the paper that said "Photographers wanted. Will train." The ad made her think about travel and interesting places and going somewhere, someplace different, and it paid $250 a week.

Eveline went for the interview, at a narrow, two-story office in an outdoor shopping mall. A man named Chuck asked her some questions, like whether she had a driver's license and had ever taken pictures before. She told him that she used to have one of the Polaroid cameras, the kind that made the picture come out right away, you didn't have to wait for it.

"I've heard worse," Chuck said.

Then he explained to her that the position was actually a baby photographer job. The photographers would drive around with heavy equipment in steel boxes, lights and tripods and a camera, and they'd go to people's houses and take pictures there. Chuck told her that the customers had all responded to an ad for a free set of 3x5 photos. After you took the photos, though, you were supposed to get them to order more, bigger pictures.

"That's where the money is," Chuck said.

On Eveline's first day, there was a big meeting. Everyone in the office was buzzing; someone important was there and was going to speak with them. The man's name was Farrell.

"Farrell's here," everybody whispered, like he was some kind of celebrity.

Farrell was a big man with greasy hair that was long and ragged looking. He wore a dull suit and a large gold pinky ring. Apparently, Farrell had made a lot of money taking baby pictures, and now he traveled around to the different company offices giving motivational speeches. Farrell stood up at the front of the room and told them that they had to take more pictures. They had to sell more pictures, even if the people didn't want more pictures.

"You have to convince them that they need photos," Farrell said. "That's your job. It doesn't matter if they're poor, I don't care if they're down to their last dime. You're salesmen."

Then Farrell started telling them about a woman named Mary Pistolesi in the New York office. Mary Pistolesi had sold more baby pictures than all of them combined. She had surpassed all the company records and won every contest. Mary Pistolesi was a genius, a prodigy. As Farrell talked about her, his face contorted with disgust. He said her name with two venomous hisses, one in the middle and one at the end.

She's not one of us, he said. You can't let yourselves be

beaten by a woman, he cried, scanning the room of aging male faces.

After that, Eveline stopped paying attention. She doodled in her notebook and pondered the strange, foreign name that had been introduced to them, "Pistolesi." She turned the name over and over in her mind like a shiny stone, examining it from every angle.

When Farrell stopped talking and the meeting was over, Chuck guided her over to a short man with a graying moustache.

"Phil's one of our best," Chuck said. "You'll apprentice with him for today, and then tomorrow you're on your own."

Phil was friendly and liked to talk. He started in as soon as they got in the car, and he didn't stop. As they drove around, he reminisced about his childhood.

"I grew up around here, and I never left," he said. "Except once to fight in Vietnam. Then I came back."

Eveline looked at him and nodded. Then Phil started talking about his friends Bobo and Kenny, and how they used to climb onto the neighborhood rooftops and throw water balloons at the people below.

"We got some of them good," he said. "We'd ambush them - they didn't know where it was coming from."

Bobo died in the war, Phil told her, and Kenny died later because of a problem with his liver.

"There were problems over there," Phil said. "Everything got all twisted up, and Kenny got twisted up along with it."

"I remember this one time," he continued. "It was after we'd swept a village. We'd fired into the huts, right through the leaves and bamboo sticks, the things they made them with.

The officers told us it was an enemy village, and we killed everyone in sight because they said we should. We killed the animals, too. Some pigs and a dog."

Phil looked at her. His voice still had a question in it after so much time.

"Anyway, after we were done, after all the sound had died down, we heard a child crying. We found him behind one of the huts, he couldn't have been more than a year old. He was lying on the ground and hugging this dead old woman, she must've been his grandmother."

Eveline turned away and stared out the window. Phil took a breath and then kept on.

"Anyway, the crying went on and on, it was the only sound you could hear in that place, everything else was so quiet. So Kenny finally went over to the kid. He picked him up and pulled him away from the grandmother. That made the kid scream even louder, he didn't want to leave the old woman. Kenny just stood there holding him for a minute, just looking at the kid like he'd never seen one before. He started screaming at the kid, "Shut up! Shut up!" But the kid kept crying, he was petrified. Then Kenny took the kid and he… he wrung its neck, right there in front of us, like it was a cat or something."

Phil stopped talking for a moment and pulled a cigarette out of his jacket pocket. His hands were shaking.

"Kenny didn't recognize himself when he got back," he said. "He couldn't live with himself, so he kept on drinking til he drank himself to death."

Eveline kept staring out the window, she couldn't think of anything to say. Wanting to drink oneself to death seemed sadly understandable given the circumstances.

They had a lot of stops that day. The first was at a small restaurant with an apartment over it. They went up the back stairs and knocked, and an Indian woman came to the door. The home smelled of spices, pungent smells that were unfamiliar to Eveline. There were two women in the apartment, a young woman and an old woman, dressed in patterned silks that draped around their waists and over their shoulders. The baby was a boy, but with long hair worn in a ponytail at the top of his head. The women readied the child for his photograph like they would a prince, caressing his arms with oil and gently arranging the bangles that adorned his wrists. With a deft, almost imperceptible motion they touched his forehead with a red mark, which shone there like a sun, like a third eye.

Eveline watched the women as they attended the child, and imagined putting on an outfit like the one they wore – the robes – and draping them across her shoulder like a Buddha. She imagined how that would feel, how it would lift your spirit up and make you feel special inside, holy. Or how it would feel to be loved in the way that baby was loved, like a god; how different the world would look then, and how much easier life would be.

After they took the pictures and left the house, Phil started talking again - this time about his wife, who had died of cancer about six months before.

"We were high school sweethearts," he said. "I didn't know anything else. I wanted to die, too."

After the Indian family they drove to another area altogether, into a rich suburb. They stopped at a large mansion, newly built on a cul-de-sac, near other mansions just like it. A pretty, well-dressed woman was home, with her baby. She looked like she had just come from the beauty parlor, Eveline thought, with very red lips and eyeshadow over her eyes. The inside of the house was white and clean, with nothing that stood out about it one way or another. The woman was married to a famous hockey player, and there were photographs on the mantle of the two of them together, on a boat. The woman was smiling in the pictures, leaning in against her husband. Her chin was tilted out to welcome the camera.

Now the woman seemed sad and lonely. After Phil took the pictures, she offered them bottles of soda and sandwiches, which Phil accepted.

Later he told Eveline – "Don't ever turn down anything that's offered you. In fact, you should always ask them to give you something, like a drink of water."

So they ate together in the big white kitchen, she and Phil and the hockey player's wife, and afterwards Eveline helped the woman with the dishes while Phil played with the baby in the living room. While they were washing and drying, passing the plates between them, the woman touched Eveline's hand. Then the woman smiled at her and it made Eveline feel a bubble in her chest.

After lunch they said goodbye to the hockey player's wife, who stood in the doorway with the baby and watched them go. She lifted the baby's little hand and made a waving motion with it, and Eveline waved back. Then she and Phil drove out of the cul-de-sac and back out onto the highway. They drove for a long time, to another, smaller suburb, where the houses were small and boxy with tiny lawns. They stopped at a worn brick rambler with a carport, and an older woman with neat, dark hair answered the door. Her expression was sad and strained, her mouth pulled downward.

The woman led them inside, where a baby gurgled in a highchair. The woman's baby had rust-colored hair and wore a white band around her head with a flower on it, and a flouncy white dress with petticoats. She wore little shoes that were made of fabric. The baby was not pretty, her features were rough and coarse. But when she smiled it made Eveline's heart ache and yearn; there was something about the baby that made her feel that way, something beautiful, something wistful and gentle. The baby's eyes were filled with peace. Eveline felt like she wanted to hold that baby, to sit with her in some quiet place, away from everyone.

There was another child there, as well – a girl of about six or seven whose name was Gia. The child haunted the corners of the room, hovering there and saying nothing. Every once in a while she looked over at the baby and hissed, pulling her lips back away from her teeth. As Phil and Eveline set up the equipment, the woman told them that she and her husband had tried for a long time to have a baby, years. They went to a lot of doctors and tried a lot of different things. Finally they had given up and adopted the little girl.

"Right after the adoption, we got pregnant," the woman said. "We wished we'd never gotten her," she whispered, nodding at Gia, "but it was too late."

Eveline looked at the little girl, who stared at the baby with hatred in her eyes. Eveline wondered what had happened to the little girl to make her so angry, whether she was angry when they found her or if she'd become angry because the woman and her husband didn't love her the way they should. Eveline tried to look ahead at the future of this family, but could see only a grim path of sorrow.

Afterwards, in the car, Phil said – "I don't know if I could feel the same way about a kid that wasn't mine. You kind of want it to be your own, right? I don't know if I could do it."

Eveline thought about the baby with the rust-colored hair and the white headband with the flower on it. She thought about her little shoes and puffy dress.

"I could," she said.

After that they drove out to the country, to the home of an older couple named Len and Ruth Carson. Len had a round belly that pressed up against his shirt buttons, and Ruth wore large glasses and a pink mu-mu. Eveline could tell right off that they were unlike the other people they had seen that day, and so could Phil. He started right in with the hard sell.

"Fifty dollars more and you get three extra 9x12s. You can have one in every room," he said.

Len and Ruth had some kind of disability that made them move slower and talk slower than other people, but after awhile Eveline couldn't see much of a difference between them and anyone else. They hovered around their baby, a little boy with a double chin and fat gathered around his wrists and ankles. They cooed over him and made little noises, and the baby grinned back at them, toothless and content.

Ruth made them lemonade and cookies, the kind that came in a loaf and you sliced them into sections. As she went back and forth between the living room and the kitchen, Len began telling stories, about when he and Ruth were kids. He said that they'd met in some kind of special school, an institution that was run by the state.

"They told our parents they would take us off their hands, that it would be better for us that way. No one knew any better back then," Len said.

Then Len told them how he'd seen kids thrown down the stairs and beaten. They'd slept two and three to a bed and were fed a kind of thin gruel that often had bugs in it, and sometimes it made the kids sick. He told them that once a kid had vomited from the gruel, and the staff made him eat the vomit.

"That's just the boys," Len said. "It was worse for the girls."

He looked at Ruth, and she looked down at her hands. Everyone knew what he meant and they just sat there for a moment, quiet, until Ruth got up and announced cheerfully that she thought the cookies were ready. No buzzer or alarm had gone off, just she thought they were ready. She disappeared into the kitchen and brought them out a few moments later, warm and piled high on a faded old dinner plate. Eveline started eating the cookies and they tasted like the best thing she'd ever had, it felt suddenly like it had been a very, very long time since she'd eaten anything that tasted good. She kept on eating them and Ruth smiled at her as she ate.

Later on, Eveline watched as Phil took the photos of the baby, who smiled and laughed with every new pose. She could tell that Phil wasn't taking as much care with the photos because he thought the Carsons wouldn't notice. Afterwards, Len picked up the baby and held him up over his head, smiling into the child's face while the child smiled back down at him, and Ruth gathered around the two of them and cooed up at the baby as well. Eveline thought about how this child was the hope that was born between them, held up like a torch against the darkness of the past.

Their next stop was the last one of the day. It was in an area Phil hadn't been to before, and he had to find it on a map. It was far out in the country, in an old mining area near Blue Bird County. The house was a small cottage, single-story, with wildflowers in the front and the shutters falling off. Eveline wondered how they'd gotten hold of the photography coupon all the way out there, it didn't look like the kind of place that had newspapers.

In the house there was an older woman with long yellow hair and several younger women, teenagers, all with yellow hair and light eyes. Maybe a mother with many daughters, Eveline thought. They were all of them barefoot, with denim pants worn thin and faded. Their eyes were quiet and clear, and they smiled gently at Eveline like they knew something about her that she didn't yet know herself, like they knew everything that awaited her in her life. None of them said anything.

There was a baby in the house but Eveline couldn't figure out who it belonged to, no one in particular seemed to claim it. They passed the child around and took turns with it, each of them equally gentle, none moreso than the others. There did not seem to be a father in the house, Eveline noticed; only the women, floating gracefully from room to room. One of them offered her a glass of something, a dark liquid, and she followed Phil's lead and drank it down, remembering what he had said about accepting what was offered you. It immediately made her feel dizzy and lightheaded.

That was all Eveline really remembered about that visit – the women and girls, barefoot in their country clothing, beautiful and mysterious. There was a feeling of great peace about the place. She helped set up the equipment and Phil took the pictures, of this baby who belonged to no one, and then they left.

On the way back to the office they got lost for awhile, and Phil had to stop and ask directions at a gas station. Eveline fell asleep with her head against the window, woozy from the alcohol. She had a dream about two rocks separating, disclosing a small tree. There was something about butterflies, too, or feathers.

When they finally got back to the shopping mall it was late, and they unloaded the car of all the equipment and carried it upstairs. There were so many metal boxes filled with lights and light stands and tripods. The equipment was so heavy that Eveline wasn't sure how she was going to manage it on her own, when they started sending her out by herself to take the photographs. Phil showed her how to do the inventory of the equipment and the film, and then they told each other goodbye.

When Eveline came back down to the parking lot, she saw Ronnie there. He had pulled cock-eye into the parking space alongside her car. He'd somehow managed to get the baby strapped into her car seat in the back, although the seat was facing the wrong way and the straps were tangled. Eveline opened the door and got into the car beside Ronnie. He was crying.

"I was sitting here," he said, "waiting for you. I thought I saw you come out the door, and I called to you, but you wouldn't come over to me. You ignored me, and you got in your car and drove away." He was weeping outright now.

"That's what I saw," he sobbed. "It must've been a dream."

The baby started gurgling and Eveline reached her hand back and rocked the car seat a little bit, gently, til the gurgling stopped and the baby let out a snore. Then Eveline brought her hand back up and put it in her lap, and she looked out the window. She suddenly felt tired and confused and like she couldn't understand what Ronnie was saying to her, and she didn't want to think about it. So she started thinking about all the people she'd seen that day instead, all the parents and all the children. She thought about the hockey player's lonely wife, touching her hand and smiling as they passed a dish between them. She thought about Phil's friend Kenny, drinking himself to death because he'd let go of his soul, and you have to fight hard to hold onto it, no matter what.

"What?" Ronnie said, tearfully. "What?"

In the back seat, the baby woke up and started to cry. Eveline reached back and loosed her from the car seat, and cradled her in her lap. For some reason, then, she found herself thinking about Mary Pistolesi. She said the name over and over in her head, and the sound of it made her feel peaceful inside. She thought about how good Mary Pistolesi had gotten at taking pictures, so good that they talked about her all the way out here, all the way in Harmon, and maybe in other places, too. Eveline could imagine her, dark and exotic with her unusual name. She imagined her far away in New York City, in a whole other world, making her way with the equipment up steep flights of tenement steps. Sounds and smells would have drifted out into the dark hallways, together with unknown languages and unknown dangers. There would have been times when she didn't make it home with her earnings, or her equipment, Eveline thought; but she'd kept on anyway. Eveline thought about how brave Mary Pistolesi must've been, and how she'd managed to carry all those heavy metal boxes, for so long, all by herself.

Ronnie grabbed for her hand and held it, but Eveline kept on looking out the window. She kept on thinking, and she didn't say anything.

Driving

They drove around that summer because there was nothing else to do. Benji had just gotten his driver's license and his father let him use his old VW bug, no air condition and a noisy engine, but it ran. They decided to look for jobs, so they drove around South Jersey scouting for places that might hire them, their shirts soaked through in the back and their legs sticking to the seats. They stopped at a bar called Kowalski's off of Route 70. It was empty in the daytime, just a guy cleaning. He had long hair and a tattoo on his neck that said "Quang Ngai." The man asked if they were 18 and shook his head "no" when they said they weren't, and then he went back to mopping the floor.

After that they stopped at an Italian restaurant called Francine's, where a woman took them down to the basement and showed them two monster-sized washing machines.

"You'd be washing the tablecloths and napkins," she explained. "The washers and dryers need to be kept going all the time."

Ginny and Benji looked around them at the heavy cinder-block walls. The room was close and dark, stifling from the heat of the dryers. Sweat had gathered at the ends of their noses and dripped onto the floor around their sneakers. Standing there, it dawned on them that there was absolutely nothing they were qualified to do at the age of 16, with no high school diplomas yet, and that washing linens continuously in a hot basement was probably all there was for them. This was so depressing that they decided to do nothing at all, and they got back into Benji's car and kept on driving.

They didn't know where to go, so Ginny directed them to the grounds of a summer camp she had attended when she was a little kid, in a quiet, rural area called Buford. It wasn't camp time yet, just the edge of summer, really, and the place was still vacant. They walked around for a long time, with Ginny narrating: This is where the nurse's office used to be, she said, this is where the bathhouse used to be. Nothing's the same now.

That was a long time ago, Benji said, and it was true. It was a long time ago, and a lot had happened in their lives since then. Ginny's mother was married to a different man now, a real bad apple. Benji's parents had become holy rollers, they watched Jerry Falwell on TV and sent him money and everything.

Benji's mother covered everything in plastic, told Benji not to touch anything, not to dirty anything. He was the child of her second marriage – her first husband had been a navy fighter pilot. They had a few children together, but then he had a heart attack and died. After that she married Benji's father, a quiet, good-hearted man who drove a forklift for a living. She didn't love him as much as she did her first husband, and he knew it.

"You're always dirty," she would tell him, when he went to

hold her hand or put his arm around her. "Your hair pomade smells like grease."

She didn't love Benji as much as her other children, either. Benji was gentle and timid like his father.

"Toughen up," she would holler, til he cried.

At night, Benji's parents would sit in matching La-Z-Boy chairs in the living room, watching Jerry Falwell and smoking. The two of them smoked so much that after awhile they were engulfed in a great cloud, shimmering and ethereal in the glow of the television. Sometimes Benji thought he could see his father's spirit hovering around him in the silver light, settling in around him like a shawl. Benji's father had emphysema, and had been warned by doctors that smoking would kill him.

"He doesn't care," Benji said. "He wants to die."

After awhile Benji moved down to the basement, where he smoked pot and took pills sometimes. He had pills of all colors. He bought a black light and began teaching himself electric guitar, like most boys do. Sometimes he thought about suicide, and he wrote in his journal – "If you hate yourself, do you have an obligation to kill yourself?"

Benji also doodled naked women in the book and wrote things like "I love girls," and "Girls are wonderful." Sometimes Benji dreamt that he was a girl. He dreamt that he was alone in unsafe places, that someone was chasing him, pursuing him, and that he was in danger.

Ginny lived in the next town over from Benji. Her mom worked at the Wawa as a night manager and her stepdad sold insurance. At night he drank a lot and went to the porno bars on Route 38, and then he came home. When Ginny was a child she would sleep on the floor of her closet when her stepdad drank, hiding, and now she didn't really go home at all.

Sometimes Ginny would sleep at Benji's house, he'd sneak her in after his parents dozed off in front of the television. He'd make up the bed for her in the guestroom, where his sister used to stay before she got married. Then Benji would lie in bed and think about Ginny in the next room, maybe lying awake herself, and he wanted to go in and lie next to her, put his arms around her, but he knew she didn't want that. Other times, when they didn't sleep at Benji's house, they would sleep at friends' houses, or stranger's houses, and even in cars sometimes, when a group of them had been out driving around all night.

Sometimes the two of them would drive to the beach in the middle of the night – no reason, just Ginny would call him up and ask, "Do you want to go to the beach?" and Benji would go get her. Sometimes, as they drove down the Parkway at midnight, Ginny would realize that she didn't want to go to the beach after all, it was something like a false alarm. She'd realize that she didn't want to be anywhere, or she didn't know where she wanted to be. Then they would pull over the car and sit there, in the darkness of the VW, and Ginny would feel herself sinking in something, like there was nothing to hold onto, like a great tide was coming in and taking her out on it.

So that was what they did that summer – they drove around in Benji's car, with no place to go. They hunted for jobs for awhile, until it dawned on them that there was nothing they wanted to do – nothing available to them that they wanted to do, anyway. So they kept on driving.

Sometimes they went to parties. They went to one by the ocean, at the home of a school friend. The parents were gone and the house was dimly lit with candles. People gathered in little clusters around the place and hovered in the yard with the beer kegs. Ginny did shots of Jack Daniels in the kitchen with a boy and two girls. Later in the evening, drunk, she slow-danced with them; the four of them in a kind of huddle, their arms around one another and their cheeks pressed close together. They stayed like that for a long time, even after the music stopped, and then one of them kissed Ginny and Ginny kissed them back. After that, Benji got drunk and took some of the pills he always carried with him in an empty tic-tac container. Then he opened an upstairs window and sat on the ledge with his feet dangling over, til Ginny made him come back in.

Sometimes Benji did things like that – he couldn't help himself. He didn't want anyone else to be close to Ginny. He wanted to be all alone in the world with her, and for her to think of him and no one else. He wanted the summer to keep on the way it had been, the two of them in his car, all alone, driving.

And it did keep on, for awhile, until the end of the summer when Ginny found out that she'd gotten a scholarship to a small college upstate, she and another boy from their class, and they drove up together for an orientation. Benji lent her the VW for the weekend, gassed up and oiled and lubed, and watched her drive away with the boy laughing in the passenger seat. Then he walked home and went down to the basement, where he played his electric guitar and took some of the red and green pills.

In the fall, Ginny went off to school, but after awhile she stopped going to class, she just wandered around the town doing nothing. There were things she'd been trying to forget that couldn't be forgotten anymore, you can't put things like that aside forever. Benji went to Parris Island as a Marine recruit but got sent home just two weeks before graduation, because he climbed up a flagpole and wouldn't come down. He just stayed up there, crying.

They didn't talk for a long time, but when Ginny came home in December she called Benji on the telephone, and they drove around in her mother's car, out to Buford and then down to the beach. Benji looked different in his new baldness, which had grown out into a kind of a crew cut, with more on top than on the sides. Although it had only been a few months, he seemed bigger, harder, more filled out. In the span of a few months, he had stopped being a boy.

Benji and Ginny didn't say much to each other, they just drove along in silence, and when they got to the beach they walked down and sat by the water, like they always did. Benji told Ginny about the flagpole and when she asked why he had done that, Benji just said that he didn't know. Ginny wanted to tell Benji things, too, but she couldn't; she didn't know the right words or even what it was that she wanted to say, or where to start, so she didn't say anything. They were just quiet and there was a sadness between them, there was nothing they could do to help one another.

They stayed by the water for a long time, and Ginny thought about how scary the ocean seemed in the darkness. She thought about how unfathomable it was, with all kinds of things lurking beneath the surface, entire worlds.

After awhile it started to rain, and they just sat there in it, getting soaked and not doing anything about it. Finally, when the lightening started, when it began playing on the waves near the jetty, they ran back to the car. Ginny got a blanket from out of the trunk, the one her mother kept there for emergencies along with the tire jack and a flashlight. Then they huddled together on the front seat and peeled off their wet clothing, shivering. They had never seen one another's bodies before, and they couldn't help but look, just for a moment, in the quiet glow of the overhead light. Then they covered themselves up.

They sat for a long time in the car, and Ginny took Benji's hand and held it. Then she gathered the blanket around her and started the car, and pulled it back onto the narrow road that led to the Parkway. There was so much pavement in front of them, and the road was so dark, and they both wished that they could keep on like that forever, driving, always in the in-between places, and never having to get where they were headed.

The Deepest, Darkest Part of the Woods

It was the summer of the bicentennial, 1976, and the country was celebrating itself. The war had been over for more than a year and things went on as ever, the children playing in the Sullivan's big back yard under skinny, century-old trees, the kind of trees with small round leaves that look like olive branches.

On most nights, fireworks could be heard in the distance, from the city, and if you climbed up high enough into an olive-branch tree you could see them rising like comets over the bridge. But apart from the frequent fireworks displays it was a summer like any other summer, like nothing had ever happened and a war had not come and gone, like nothing had been altered forever. Into the heart of the neighborhood the last of the soldiers had returned, they let their hair grow long and disguised themselves as ordinary boys.

Bobby Campo came home that summer, after most of the others, to his parents' house on the bulb of the cul-de-sac. The doctors had kept him at the VA for a long time, with multiple operations to repair a leg that was severed at the torso. After six surgeries they declared that the leg was saved, but warned that it would never be right. It attached to his body like a battered broom handle, skinny and atrophied from months of disuse and patch-worked with skin grafts. Certain muscles and tendons had been damaged and could not be repaired. Bobby dragged the leg behind him like an afterthought when he walked.

When Bobby came back, he felt like he was nowhere. The world around him seemed far away, like he was seeing everything from a great distance, from within a bubble of some kind. The neighborhood looked nothing like he remembered it, everything seemed very still, like a photograph or a painting instead of something real. It left him feeling empty inside and lonely. He hadn't thought it would be that way.

Most of the time, Bobby stayed inside, in his room. He felt like a stranger there, spying on the life of some other boy. There were posters of cars on the wall and sketches of a comic book character who appeared to be made out of rocks, and another who wore a flag-colored bodysuit. There were the beginnings of a coin collection, things the other boy had cared about.

Sometimes Bobby would leave the house to go to the grocery store, or the billiards place. "Billiards and Pool," it said on the outside. Or sometimes he would walk down to the high school, Bishop Eustis. There was a plaque in the front entranceway with the names of boys on it, graduates who'd gone to the war and been killed. Bobby knew some of them. There was a guy named Shaggy whose real name, Richard, was on the plaque. Shaggy was tall and gangly with a large forehead and a funny, compressed face. He wore his hair pulled back in a tiny ponytail that looked like the end of a paintbrush. And Randy Baggio – a kid they called Slug – his name was on the plaque, too. Slug was a sullen, skinny kid who'd spent time in a juvenile detention facility after the police caught him drowning cats in a nearby creek. Slug was made for war, Bobby thought; the kind of person who went over and discovered himself there, in the shadow of the heaviest, deepest jungle, liberated to his most brutal instincts. Slug was the kind of person who didn't want to come home from war, Bobby thought, and he hadn't.

Sometimes Bobby would walk the halls of the high school, after hours. The janitor would meet him at the back door and let him in, and they'd smoke a joint together in the supply closet. The janitor had been with some kind of special unit in the war, and he had a tattoo on his neck that said "Born to Die." After they smoked, the janitor would pull out his needle and works and Bobby would leave him there, strangling his arm with a rubber tube. Then Bobby would travel the empty corridors alone, slowly to accommodate his weakened leg, and he'd peer into the classrooms and maybe try the lock on his old locker. His ghost lingered in the school like a shadow, with shorter hair and a fuller, softer face, and he could see himself there as he had been.

Occasionally, in the afternoons, Bobby would sit on the front porch and watch the neighborhood children at their rituals. Across the street, a group of them would gather and play in a ditch, digging with plastic shovels and garden spades. There did not seem to be a goal or a reason for it. Roaches or beetles of some kind would scurry out by the dozens, and the kids would squash and stomp on them as quickly as they could. Stevie D'Ambrosio would crush them between his fingers, laughing, and the other kids would use their sneakers. Sometimes Stevie would come out of the house and play in the ditch in just his underwear, and his dad would come looking for him and beat him with a board, right there in front of everyone.

Sometimes the kids would gather at the home of the hippie, a pretty woman who'd moved to the neighborhood just a few months before. The hippie called herself Cassandra, which was a name she'd taken from Greek mythology. Cassandra had the gift of prophesy, she told the children; the problem was that no one would believe those prophesies. The children agreed that this was unfortunate.

Cassandra smoked pot on her front porch and gave the children candy. She issued each of them an animal name, depending on which animal she thought they most resembled. She was an artist, and would paint large, bright canvases, mostly nudes, all of which bore the phrase – "I wanted a canary, but a caged bird never sings."

Every once in awhile Cassandra would invite the children into her living room, with their dirty hands and popsicle drippings down their fronts, and band-aids with cherry-colored mercurochrome seeping out from underneath. She'd let them look through her record collection, which was mostly Rolling Stones. The kids liked the album cover that had a man's zipper on it. Or sometimes she'd make them lie down on the floor and she'd put on her meditation record, which was a man's voice telling you to relax every part of your body, from your feet all the way up to the top of your head. Usually the kids would fall asleep during this exercise, leaving behind small puddles of drool. Other times they'd gather around her on the couch, perch on its back like gargoyles, and she'd read their palms and tell them what life had in store for them. She told Stevie D'Ambrosio that he didn't have a very long lifeline.

Sometimes Bobby would see the woman watching him as he limped around the neighborhood, and her gaze seemed sad, like she felt sorry for him, and he'd feel his face grow hot with embarrassment. Sometimes she'd wave to him, wave him over, but he ignored her.

On some days, when Bobby got tired of watching the children digging in the ditch or hovering around Cassandra, he'd go over to the trailer park, where his friend Tony Coyle lived. He and Tony had been best friends since they were little kids. Tony had lived in the trailer all his life, with his mother – he was gentle and quiet and used to play the accordion. He didn't play anymore since he got home from the war, he just sat in the trailer and watched television, and he looked at Bobby like he didn't know him. Tony's mother would bring them glasses of lemonade and ginger snaps, placing the tray silently on the table beside Tony. Her face was drawn and dark with grief, fallen in on itself like a crumpled newspaper. Then Bobby and Tony would sit and look at the TV together.

In the evenings, Bobby's sisters would have girls over to the house, and they would flirt with Bobby's younger brother, Davie. Davie had long, sandy hair, and wore the kind of wire-framed glasses that were dark at the top of the lenses and lighter at the bottom. He was different from Bobby, good-looking and charismatic. Davie went to the local parochial school, Camden County Vo-Tech, where they taught him how to take engines apart. He had planned on enlisting and was disappointed when the war ended.

"I was gonna kick their asses for what they did to Bobby!" He would say.

Most of the girls who came to the house were 15 or 16, Bobby's sisters' ages. They seemed loud and crude to Bobby, and sometimes one or another of them would go into the bedroom with Davie and shut the door. There was one girl who was younger, 12 or 13, maybe. She was quiet, with long hair pulled back in a braid and skin a light ochre color. The darkness of her hair made him think of other girls he had seen, someplace else, and he found himself looking for the girl when the children gathered to play their various games of tag in the cul-de-sac. When he saw her, he thought of another girl, a girl who had shaken and cried as they searched her family's small hovel. She had knelt on the ground with her father and mother, their hands in the air. Her fear had pierced and sickened him, filled him with a self-loathing that he would carry with him everywhere he went, like a shameful secret.

Bobby thought of another time, too, when he'd watched as some men dragged a pretty young girl with black hair into a shack. He'd heard her screams, her pathetic pleading; they were sounds that he never could have imagined, that tore something inside of him in a way that was violent and jagged, and something in his head broke away and went someplace else forever. Afterwards, there were no more screams and just silence. Bobby had stood there, dumbly, his hands sweating on his rifle. The men looked at him and laughed when they emerged from the hut. Bobby thought of that day when he looked at the neighborhood girl.

The Deepest, Darkest Part of the Woods

Bobby knew the girl's father, a man named Waddell. He had cut the grass for Waddell a few summers before, it seemed like forever ago now, like it was a different person altogether who had cut that grass. Waddell was stern, humorless. He wore overalls and chopped wood in the yard, and the neighborhood kids called him Daniel Boone. His wife was from the Philippines, people said, a mail-order bride.

Rumor had it that Waddell was a drunk, a behind-closed-doors drunk. People heard things coming from the house sometimes, at night. Bobby's sister spied in the windows once, and saw Waddell spit something into the girl's mouth, gin or something, when she went to kiss him goodnight. The girl always looked sad and lonesome, Bobby thought. The neighborhood kids called her gook and slope. Sometimes Bobby wanted to yell out to her, to say something comforting, but he didn't.

Still, Bobby kept watching for the girl. He watched her planting things in Waddell's garden with her mother, and cutting the grass in Waddell's big yard, struggling with the mower. He watched when she came home one day with a new bicycle, from the big Goodwill store on Route 38. It was silver and shiny with red writing on it. She rode it around the neighborhood, fast like a blur. Joey Martone, a scrawny kid with a crew cut and scabs all over his legs from picking mosquito bites, tried to keep up on his brother's three-speed.

"Is that a ten-speed?" He asked, when she beat him.

"No," she said. "It's just regular."

Shortly after that, Joey and Stevie and some other kids sneaked into the Waddell's shed and stole the bike. They dismantled it and threw the parts into the creek behind the housing development.

Sometimes the girl would catch Bobby watching her, and she would look back at him for a moment, and then return to whatever she was doing. Once, when she came over to the house, the girl brought Bobby a coin. She came into his bedroom quietly and put it on his desk, and then she left. It was an old Indian head nickel, a rare one. Bobby wondered where she had found it, and why she had given him such a gift, and how she'd known that he had once collected coins.

It was sometime after that when Bobby had a dream about the girl. In the dream he was some kind of a spirit, a ghost. Imperceptible and weightless, he entered the Waddell home through a thin crack at the top of the front door. He floated into the living room, where he hovered on the ceiling. Mrs. Waddell sat on the couch below him, crying. Then Bobby drifted into the children's room, through a keyhole. The girl was there, along with her younger brother, still a toddler. In the dream, Bobby made his body re-materialize and he picked up the children, one in each arm. They continued sleeping, their heads against his shoulder. Then Bobby started to run. He ran through a wilderness carrying the children. The girl hugged his neck tightly, her black hair flying loose, her cream-colored skin damp against his shoulder. She smelled like wet leaves. As Bobby ran up the hill and toward the road he could feel Waddell behind him, gaining on him, so close that he could hear his labored breathing. He could feel Waddell's hands grasping at his ankle.

There were so many things to dream about. Often, Bobby dreamt in a jumble of different languages, struggling with them throughout the night, trying to understand what was being said to him, or asked of him. Sometimes he dreamt about things that had happened, things he had done and seen, re-living them over and over as if the outcome, the course of events, might change with repetition.

Other times, Bobby would dream about God. In one dream, God wore a black hat and carried a shotgun, like some kind of a hillbilly, Bobby thought. God told him something like – "Go to the deepest, darkest part of the woods, and you'll find me there." So Bobby did. He ran through the woods and forest and jungle, until he came to a small clearing, filled with sunlight. God was there, wearing his black hat. He lifted the shotgun to his eye, and pointed it at Bobby.

The dream seemed odd to Bobby, because he'd never thought of God that way, and couldn't imagine God carrying a gun or wanting to hurt him. Bobby thought about the dream for a long time, puzzled over it, and it wasn't until years later, when his life was different and the cul-de-sac was very far away, that he thought perhaps he understood it.

As the summer drew on, Bobby took to sitting on the roof and watching the kids play their games of jailbreak in the neighbor's yard. He'd climb out from his bedroom window and prop up on the slope, his feet braced against the gutter. In the twilight, Bobby would see flashes of white as the children gave chase to their enemies. Sometimes he'd lie there on his back, watching the pinpoint of his cigarette glowing red and then dying out with each breath. He felt peaceful then, watching for things and listening, and hearing the night sounds as they swelled - crickets, locusts, whippoorwills. Sometimes he'd look over at the Waddell's house. Often, the kitchen was illuminated and he could see the stark figures of Waddell and his wife, sitting at opposite ends of the table.

One night, from his rooftop perch, Bobby saw the girl leaving the house. She was wearing a quilted pink bathrobe. She went into the shed where they kept the lawnmower and the garden tools. Bobby thought perhaps he was imagining her, it was such a strange place for her to be, and he strained to watch the shed in the darkness. After that, Bobby would watch for the girl every evening, and sometimes he would see her - leaving the house stealthily, in the deepest nighttime.

Sometime around Independence Day, Stevie D'Ambrosio lit a fire in his bedroom and the ambulance came and took him away, first to the hospital and then to to some kind of home for unwanted children. After that, the rest of the children became withdrawn and sullen. Their hair and fingernails grew long and dirty and they wore the same clothing for days on end. They set up camps down by the old polluted creek and slept there, they wouldn't go home. The parents relinquished the children to this wildness, engrossed in their own sweltering, mid-summer affairs and flirtations. In the evenings, they lit hibachis and propped their stereos in the windows, and danced with one another's husbands and wives until dawn.

The hippie joined in from afar – she sat outside on her stoop every night, smoking pot and reading fortunes with a special set of cards with pictures on them. Davie pulled one that had a picture of a man hanging upside-down by his foot, and she told him it meant that there would be a great change in his life.

Toward the end of July, Tony Coyle walked up onto the highway overpass and jumped down into the traffic below.

Someone who saw it said that he had sat on the railing for awhile, quiet, and then let himself fall backwards onto the hood of an oncoming car. Bobby went to the funeral, which was held at the local cemetery off of Route 38, the one they'd passed every day on the bus ride to and from school. There was a white, life-sized Jesus hanging from a cross at the front gate. His face looked delicate and pained. Over his head it said "INRI," and Bobby wondered what that meant.

During the service, some boys rode by on their bikes, and they stopped and watched through the fence as the casket was lowered into the earth. Tony's mother let out a bleating kind of a cry, like a sheep or something, not a sound a person would make.

Sometime after that, some kids came over from Montrose Street and beat Davie unconscious, because he'd been caught with somebody's sister. They had found them together in an abandoned car behind the Acme, where Davie worked as a bag boy. So now the boys circled Davie on the street while the rest of the children hid in the darkness at the edge of the Sullivan's yard.

"We're going to kill you, boy," one of them said to Davie. There was something like a board or a club in his hand.

They beat him until there was blood coming from his nose and mouth.

In August, they brought Davie home from intensive care. His long, sandy hair and his two-toned glasses were gone. To make his mother feel better, Bobby let her drive him down to the community college.

"You're so smart, Bobby," she said. "Please."

Bobby stood in line at the registrar's office. He felt like

people were looking at him and could see where he'd been and all the things he'd done. The boys and girls around him seemed weightless, foolish, trite – they clustered together in groups and laughed at nothing. But here and there he saw boys who had the same distant, sad look that he had. Their clothes were baggy and ill-fitting, outdated. They hovered in the line alone, uncertain, detached.

On one of the last days of the summer, Labor Day, the neighborhood had its annual picnic. Bobby felt lonely and called a friend who had also just come home, but who was miles away in California. The boy had no legs anymore. He sounded happy to hear from Bobby, and they both let out loud whoops and chatted rapidly for a minute or two, like two people clinging to one another and nothing else. But then the boy grew listless again, and Bobby felt himself start to feel heavy inside and tired. Then the boy told him about one of their friends who'd come home with burns all over his body, and another who'd taken an overdose of painkillers he'd been hoarding in his nightstand at the VA. Then they got off the phone.

Afterwards, Bobby went out onto the porch and watched as the children ran in the twilight. He could hardly remember what it felt like to run for the joy of running, without a reason to run, the wild surge of ecstasy. He felt like he was watching through a filter or a membrane of some kind, which made him feel separate from everything around him. From his distant place, he watched as the children joined in packs, chasing, hiding, searching. He could see the girl as she darted around the yard, her long braid flying behind her, her strides smooth and graceful. From somewhere, music began playing, Steppenwolf and the Doors, and you could hear the parents laughing and talking as they gathered in someone's backyard, their glasses making tinkling sounds as they filled them. The evening went on like that, with the music, and the parents kept on drinking.

Later that night, Bobby sat on the rooftop. He watched as the last of the neighborhood revelers went inside. One couple was drunk and groped one another loudly; it was the widow of the Air Force pilot and a man he recognized from church, he could hear them both giggling. From across the yard Bobby could see Waddell, too, sitting on his back porch, the glint of a glass in his hand as it rose to his lips and fell back again, watching as the couple embraced on the widow's front lawn. After a long time Waddell stood up, put his hands in his pockets, and looked out into the darkness of his yard. Then he turned around and went inside, and closed the door behind him.

Bobby sat on the rooftop until long after the sky grew black and the lights in nearly all the homes on the cul-de-sac went out. He waited until the lights in Waddell's home went out, last of all, after Waddell stood up from the kitchen table. He waited until the night reached its peak and achieved a great loneliness, the moment when the imprint of humanity was absent and the night sounds overtook and consumed the world. It was then that Bobby saw what he had hoped to see: the girl, exiting the house quietly, and creeping toward the shed. As he watched her, he thought about how she sat in the shed at night, with the lawnmower and garden tools around her, and the smell of cut grass. He imagined that she made herself small in the growing darkness, listening and watching, the aloneness pressing in around her.

It was Bobby's intention to leave the rooftop that night, to shimmy down the drainpipe and cross the lawn, his bad leg keeping up with his good leg. He imagined himself entering the shed and seeing the girl there, crouched in the corner in her quilted bathrobe. She would look at him unsurprised, like she'd been waiting for him, like she'd been watching him, too, and she'd put a finger gently to her lips in the "hush" sign.

Bobby imagined that he would sit down several feet away from the girl, so as not to scare her. He would sit quietly near the entrance to the shed, and draw his knees up to his chest. The crickets would hum, and the squirrels and night birds would make their sounds, forest sounds, and after awhile she would fall into a peaceful sleep, her cheek against the cool cement floor.

And no one would dare come near them like that, Bobby thought – and he would wait and watch as the night passed over and around them, like a stream around stones.

Graduation

That summer, Billy and Maryellen and I graduated from high school. Maryellen had plans to be a computer operator and Billy was taking classes in auto shop. I worked at a Dunkin' Donuts down the street from where I lived, to save money for college. My mother's husband, Frank, would come in for lunch sometimes, he'd order soup and coffee and then watch us waitresses as we worked. Frank spent most of his time at the porno bars near our house, drinking. Then he came home.

Frank had a sister named Mel who was crazy. She chain-smoked and her mouth moved all the time, but no words came out. Frank told us that when she was 13 their father had taken her bedroom door off the hinges, so he could watch her dress and undress. When she was 18 she stabbed the father in the back with a grapefruit knife. After that they put her in a hospital and fried her brain until she forgot why she'd wanted to stab him in the first place.

Mel had come to stay with us once, when she was pregnant

with twins. The doctors thought there was something wrong with the babies and they wouldn't live, they were dying inside of her. Her boyfriend had kicked her out of their apartment. She stayed with us for a few weeks, chain smoking in the living room, until Frank told her she had to leave.

"She's going to burn the house down," he said.

So Mel went home, back to her boyfriend in California. A few weeks later she tried to kill herself with the car running in a closed garage.

Sometime after that I found a copy of Mel's high school yearbook in our basement. She was in all the pictures: yearbook staff, class treasurer, varsity basketball manager. She had a wide smile and a kind of quietness about her. The book was filled with signatures, covered with them. One of them said "To our pretty little blue eyes. Stay as sweet as you are."

On most nights I stayed over at Maryellen's house, I never wanted to go home. Maryellen's father was a bass player with a band down in Atlantic City, at one of the casinos. Sometimes he'd wake us up when he got home from a gig, and he'd put on his "Porgy and Bess" album and sing to us. Maryellen's mother would join in with him, sometimes. She was from the South and I liked the way her voice sounded when she sang.

Billy was my boyfriend, kind of. His parents were divorced and his father had remarried a skinny woman with yellow hair. His mother saw a guru who told her only to wear red next to her skin and not to concern herself with worldly things. So she didn't, and their kitchen countertops were piled high with dirty dishes and pots, and the cats ate out of the sink.

Billy had a younger sister named Celeste who went everywhere with us. Billy used to get her to flush the toilet while he started his mom's car and rolled it down the driveway, to cover the noise. One time I went over there to wait for Billy to get home from work, and Celeste put a record on and asked me to dance with her. Another time, when I went over for dinner, she held my hand under the table while Billy held my other hand.

Billy worked the night shift at a convenience store. One night when he was riding his bike home from work he got hit by a car. The driver was a girl about our age, it was her first time taking the car out by herself. The accident snapped Billy's arm in two and they had to do all kinds of skin grafts and bone grafts to try and save it. For a long time the skin grafts wouldn't take and the arm took on a raw, purplish color, and then it started to turn a pale green. They had all kinds of drains and tubes going in and out of it, but Billy's doctor said that the arm was starting to die.

After that, Billy didn't sleep much anymore. He'd just drive around all night in his mother's car, thinking about his dying arm. Or sometimes he'd pick us up and we'd all drive down to the beach together, and we'd lie together on the sand and watch the sun come up. There was something about watching the morning come that made me feel all alone and like I was sinking in something, like a stone being dropped down a deep, dark well. I felt afraid inside and I wondered "What will happen to me?"

After Billy hadn't slept for about two months he decided to check himself into the hospital. He was on a ward with a guy who'd almost jumped off the Walt Whitman Bridge and a girl who drank Windex. When I went to visit him once I saw a girl being restrained by some orderlies in the parking lot. It took five of them to hold her down, one on each limb and another who sat on her back.

In June, Billy got out of the hospital. Maryellen found out she was pregnant and decided to have an abortion. The night before the operation we stayed out all night with a bottle of Coco-Ribe, with Maryellen crying, and Billy gave us little pieces of paper to chew that made everything move like slow motion. Then we drove to the empty Ken-Mart parking lot and lay on the hood of the car, looking up.

A few weeks later, we all finally graduated. Billy's mom was there in her red mu-mu, and Maryellen's dad gave us each a card that said – "The odyssey has begun – take it and run!" I looked at it and wondered what he was thinking. I read a poem I had written, but I didn't read it loud enough and afterwards some people said they couldn't hear. A math teacher made a speech, something about how we wouldn't be the people who would change the world, but how somehow that was okay. After the ceremony we drove to somebody's house for a party. On the way there I sat on Celeste's lap, and she kept rubbing my knee the whole way.

I remember the next day we took a trip to the beach, to Asbury Park. Maryellen's mother lent us her brand-new beach chairs and made Maryellen swear that she'd bring them back. When we got there we walked on the boards, and then we stopped at a fortune teller. She told me that I had a spot on my aura and for five extra dollars she'd remove it. Then she told me that somebody far away wanted to see me. I liked to think about that. Somebody far away. Wanting to see me.

Later on, Billy tried to throw Maryellen in the water, because he didn't know that you can't be in water for a certain amount of time after an abortion. I tried to stop him, and we wound up pulling on Maryellen's arms like she was a doll. After that nobody really said too much, we just sat on the blanket and looked at the ocean. We thought about the future, which was like a dark place opening up before us. Then we left.

On the way home we got a flat, and Billy had to change the tire using just one hand, no one else knew how to do it. We drove back to Maryellen's house with the windows rolled down. Everyone was quiet, we were all together but we were completely apart, and a deep loneliness came over us with the darkness.

When we finally got home that night we realized that we had picked up and left the beach chairs sitting by the water, just like that, like we were coming back or something.

Median

They called Wendell at home that morning. It was before he left for work, and he was sitting at the kitchen table having his breakfast. His wife was sitting next to him, wearing a housecoat that was quilted like a blanket. She had recently retired from her job as a music teacher at the elementary school, and Wendell was getting ready to retire from his job, too. They were going to do what everyone did when they retired - take a few trips, visit with relatives, maybe see the Grand Canyon. His wife wanted to visit the Four Corners, too–the place where New Mexico, Arizona, Utah and Colorado all converge, a place where there is supposed to be some kind of great magic. His wife believed in magic. She felt it all the time, she said, all around her. She longed to see and be near places that had magic.

That morning, the telephone rang while he was eating toast. It was Mel Fisher on the line.

"I was just on my way into the office," Wendell said. "Is something wrong?"

"Something is wrong," Mel said. Mel was the sheriff.

"There was a crash off of Route 53, a bus crash," he said. "Some kids on their way back from a school trip to Petersburg. They went off the overpass and onto the highway. You should come down."

"I'll come down right now," Wendell said. His voice sounded like it was coming from someplace else.

When he hung up the phone, his wife was looking at him.

"What is it?" She asked.

"There's been an accident," Wendell said. "A school bus. They were on their way back from a trip or something."

Wendell stood up and put his jacket on. It was a beautiful morning with a blue sky and warm, but he put on his jacket anyway.

Usually, Wendell's job involved more typical, straightforward events - a heart attack here and there, or someone falling off a ladder. Every once in a while, a suicide, maybe, and those were the hardest. There was a man who ran the local bicycle shop who shot himself. He had no wife, no relatives, so they just locked up the shop and left it, as-is. When you walked by you could still see all the merchandise in the window, crowded in and piled from the floor to the ceiling. It's a shame, Wendell thought, all those bicycles going to waste.

Sometimes it was a young person who did that, who ended their life. There was a boy they found in the woods, hanging from a tree, and a girl they found in a motel bathroom. Wendell could still remember the motel room, shabby and dark. A single cigarette had been left in the ashtray, haphazardly extinguished, and the television had been left on. An unfathomable anguish hung in the air and pressed down upon him. Wendell thought about the girl for weeks afterwards. He thought about her life, and the betrayal of it. She had not been born only to die in that manner, Wendell thought, broken and destroyed.

When Wendell was a child, he'd been told that people who did that went to hell, but he didn't believe that. God wasn't like that, he thought. In fact, God would love them best of all – the lost, the abandoned, the irretrievable. The people for whom life had been a process of coming apart, rather than coming together.

When Wendell told his wife about those calls, about the man with the bicycle shop and the girl in the motel bathroom, she put her hand on his arm.

"God can't necessarily stop us from suffering," she said, softly. "Didn't Jesus suffer? We're not supposed to not suffer."

Wendell's wife was religious, she believed in the afterlife. She believed in things like angels. She enjoyed watching television shows about people who saw angels, or about people who died on the operating table and then came back to life. There was one story about a man who was dead for a number of minutes, and during that time he went into a bright light. He said that while he was in the light he was filled with a great love and peace, and he saw and understood everything, everything was clear to him. When he came back he had gifts and abilities he hadn't had before. He was suddenly a great mathematician. He could play Brahms on the piano.

"I wouldn't mind that," Wendell said to his wife.

There was another show about a boy whose father would tie him to a pole in their basement and beat him. On one occasion when this was happening, an angel appeared to the boy. He stood behind the father, cloaked in golden light. He was larger than life, the boy later reported. After that day, the TV program said, the father never hurt the child again.

This story confused Wendell. Why did some people see angels, and others didn't? God couldn't love some people more than others, Wendell thought. That wouldn't be right. Wendell often found himself thinking about those stories, about how it would be to have an angel appear to you, or to cross over into great light, and how nothing would be the same after that.

Anyway, his wife loved that kind of thing now, those kinds of stories. Anything out of the ordinary. She loved the ones where people would suddenly get superhuman strength, too, like the mother whose son got pinned under a car and she lifted it off of him.

"It's not like she picked up the car and held it over her head," his wife explained. "Life is not a cartoon. She was just able to lift the back corner enough so that her son could breathe."

His wife paused for a moment, then continued. "People can do extraordinary things under those circumstances," she said. "A parent can do that kind of thing to save a child."

Wendell reached over and touched her hand when she said that.

They told Wendell and his wife that their son had been a hero. Someone had thrown some kind of explosive into a crowded market, and while everyone else scattered his son had jumped on top of it, and it blew a hole through his chest. Wendell thought about his son like a stranger after that. What would possess a human being to do such a thing, he wondered. The act seemed so incongruous with the child he had known; a good boy, but not an unusual boy, not an extraordinary boy.

Median

His son was average - he played electronic games and watched television. He played the guitar badly. He had pimples and enjoyed dressing in a slovenly fashion. But in the short time that his son had been away, he had changed. He had become someone else.

That's one of the reasons kids join the military, his wife explained. They want meaning. In that moment, she said, our son found his meaning.

Wendell felt confounded. He couldn't make peace with it the way his wife tried to do. He felt numb and bewildered. We raised that boy, he thought. A lot of time and work went into raising that boy, for it to all be gone so soon.

His son lived for three days, at the army hospital in Germany. His face and chest were smothered in bandages. There were tubes going in and out.

Wendell's wife said - He has a mortal wound. You're not supposed to survive a mortal wound. It means that you're forever in an in-between state. His soul can't rest, she said. He can't be free. Wendell thought he knew what she meant.

I had a dream, his wife told him. The night it happened. This is not unusual, she told him. A lot of parents and loved ones have such dreams. I dreamt that our son was walking in a dangerous place, and I wanted to stop him. I wanted him to stand still. I called to him but he didn't hear me.

His wife told him that she'd had another dream, too, several nights later, after their son had died. He came to her and kissed her on the cheek. He was wearing the bathrobe she had bought him, the one with brown and black horses on it. He was smiling.

It scared me a little, his wife confessed. But it made me happy, too.

War Stories

Wendell didn't have a dream. He wanted to have a dream, but he didn't. He went to work and came home, like always. At night he would sit at the edge of the bed and stare at the wall in front of him. He felt like he wasn't there, like he was a ghost entering and leaving the house. After the funeral, his wife put the flag on the mantle, shaped into a perfect, squat triangle. I wonder how they do that? Wendell thought.

That morning, after he got the call from Mel, Wendell drove out toward the crash site. He passed open fields and dense stands of trees. Here and there, a farmhouse. Telephone lines were strung overhead, connecting everything. After awhile, in the distance, Wendell could see a cloud of gray smoke rising from behind a cluster of trees. The smoke was heavy and dark, menacing. It traveled into the atmosphere with ferocity, making a black funnel up to the sky. As he watched it, Wendell thought about a day a long time ago, years ago, when he was a child. He and his parents had been traveling on a one-lane, country road between Woodville and Franklin. They were on their way home from his grandparents' house, and his mother sang in the front seat, like she always did. The window was down and her hair blew across her face and into her eyes and mouth. Her legs were folded beneath her and her slip was showing, and she seemed free and careless, like a young girl. But when she shifted her weight and her slip moved upward, Wendell could see purple bruises on her thighs, and it made him feel dull and weighted down inside. Wendell's father had his arm out the window, his hand holding a cigarette. He looked annoyed with his mother's singing, but his mother was happy and pretended not to care, she pretended that the journey home would take forever, and they would never have to arrive.

Median

At some point on the way home, Wendell remembered, his father had fallen asleep at the wheel. The car veered off the road, crashing through the tree line and into a quarry. They landed upside-down at the bottom, and silence engulfed them. The three of them hung in the overturned vehicle, suspended by their seatbelts, not moving. His mother's hair streamed behind her and his father's head rested lightly on his seatback. Everything was quiet in the car except for a moaning sound that someone was making. It occurred to Wendell then just how fast everything could change, in only one moment.

Wendell hung there for a long time, the gash in his forehead bleeding into his hair and turning it black and matted. He felt a great loneliness pressing in around him, crushing his chest and filling him with despair. After awhile some clouds gathered, and heat lightening flickered in the distance, and Wendell let himself fall into a deep sleep and dream. He saw himself traveling down a narrow river, in what must have been a small rowboat. There were red clay banks on either side of the river, and the trees arched gently overhead, creating a dense canopy. The sound of the water was soft against the bow of the boat.

After a long time, a car passed by. Wendell woke up from his dream and heard a man's voice, gentle and baritone. He felt someone cutting him free from the seatbelt, carrying him away from the crumpled car and laying him softly in the grass at the side of the road. Wendell opened his eyes for a moment and saw the silhouette of the man's hat, the round brim. The sun was behind him and his face was obscured in shadow.

When Wendell awoke in the hospital, he asked about the man who had pulled him from the car. He was a businessman from up North, they told him, a Yankee, just passing through.

When Wendell arrived at the crash site that morning, Mel was there to meet him. The bus had plunged 200 feet over a cement barrier and lay where it fell, disfigured and gnarled like a crushed aluminum can. It looked as though a powerful giant had been walking down the interstate and stepped on it, grinding it into the cement with its heel. The fuel tanks had exploded with the impact, and the fire fighters were still putting out the flames.

"There are children in there," Mel said. "There are a few who were thrown, but it doesn't look good."

Mel led him around the site, through the police and firefighters and paramedics. Here and there, bodies lay like piles of crumpled rags. Wendell stopped at each one, leaning over the backs of the EMTs. Around them, on the pavement, were articles of clothing – underwear, socks, blue jeans – things that must have come loose from the suitcases. He saw a shirt hanging from a nearby tree and a bottle of shampoo and some tweezers on the ground. There was a smell in the air that made Wendell feel sick to his stomach. Parents were starting to gather behind the yellow tape that the officers had strung between two police cruisers, they were wailing and shouting.

From a distance, Wendell heard someone calling him. He turned to where Mel was standing, gesturing at a figure on the ground. As Wendell approached, he saw a boy lying on the asphalt—his face and head were bloody and his body was twisted, but Wendell could see that the boy was still breathing, faintly. Mel was looking at him, a desperate "Well?" in his eyes.

Wendell knelt on the ground next to the boy. He could see that there was nothing to be done, they could all see that, but Wendell got down on the ground beside the boy anyway. People seemed to be expecting something. He opened his bag. He put his face near the boy's mouth and listened to the respirations, so shallow that he could barely feel them against his cheek. He started CPR, and the sweat ran into his eyes and down his back as he worked, alternating breaths and compressions. After awhile, Wendell stopped and held the boy's wrist again, his own heart pounding with the unaccustomed exertion. Wendell could feel the boy's pulse fluttering and fading, and then it stopped altogether.

The boy's eyes were open and his sneaker lay on the pavement near Wendell's feet. From behind the yellow tape rushed a man and woman who threw themselves on the boy, wailing. Wendell moved away to let them through. He picked up the sneaker and walked to the median and sat down. He felt dizzy and empty inside, and he put his head down on his arms for a long time. He listened to the parents weep, and he felt sorry for them.

After it was all over, and the last of the ambulances had departed, screaming, and the flames had been extinguished, Wendell got up to go. He walked back to his car, carrying his battered medicine bag. His feet ached as he walked, and he felt a deep tiredness coming over him.

Wendell opened the car door and sat in the driver's seat, unmoving. Eventually, he started the engine and began to drive. As he pulled his car out onto the highway from where it had been parked on the shoulder, he noticed that someone had been left behind: a solitary young man in a grey sweatshirt sat alone in the median, pulling a dandelion apart in his hands. A light rain began to fall and the boy pulled the hood of his sweatshirt over his head, and stuffed his hands in his pockets.

Why was he still there, Wendell wondered? Where were

his parents? Wendell rolled down the window and called to the boy, but his words were lost and weak in the sound of the traffic. When the boy looked up Wendell could see that his expression was calm, like he was waiting for someone he knew would arrive. He lifted a hand to Wendell, waving him on in an "I'm okay" gesture. Wendell raised his hand in return, and the boy nodded. Then Wendell pulled out onto the highway. A moment later his mobile rang, it was his wife.

"Is everything alright?" she asked.

Later, Wendell sat in his chair in the living room while his wife fixed dinner. She brought him a small glass of a sweet wine, sherry, and he stared at the fireplace although there was no fire lit. As he sat there, Wendell thought about the day that had passed and let it unwind in his head the way he always did. He thought about the shirt hanging from the tree and the smell in the air. He thought about the parents wailing in the kind of grief that seems to have no end. And as Wendell closed his eyes and began to drift into a light sleep, he thought about the young man on the median, and how his form had receded in the rear view mirror. Wendell thought about how there was something familiar about the boy, something that reminded him of something else, although he was sure this was a boy he didn't know at all.

Love Spell

Did I tell you about the time I went to visit my friend Callie in Fort Bloom? I took the train all the way out into Brooklyn, to the very end of the line - so far that you think you must be in another city already, another place altogether. The subway car empties and quiets with each stop, until no one gets on or off and you begin to feel like you're racing into nowhere or crossing some kind of gap in the universe, all alone, with just the screaming and scraping of the train gears. That's how it felt to me, anyway - like the train to the farthest reaches of Brooklyn was taking me into another dimension entirely.

In Fort Bloom, there were vagrants on the sidewalk and the abandoned lots were strewn with trash. The doors and windows of the houses were boarded and the grass had grown wild, that's what the neighborhood was like back then. It looked as though the people who had lived there once had long since vanished, forced out by a plague or a disaster of some kind.

Callie was living in a broken-down rooming house on Jones Street, with crumbling steps and a roof that bowed inward. Inside, the house was dark and quiet, cave-like. The floor and carpet were rotted and the hallways smelled of mildew. Callie said there were other people living there, but I didn't see them.

Callie's apartment was big enough for a mattress on the floor and a dresser. There was a small sink built into the wall and a hotplate in the corner, and there were clothes and shoes all over the floor. The walls were peeling and it looked as though past tenants had written on them, like prisoners would do. Callie said that it used to be a drug house, a place where addicts would gather, and long before that it had been inhabited by Eastern European immigrants and their sewing machines.

Callie and I lived in the same place, in the same town, and in fact, the same apartment before she moved to Brooklyn and I moved someplace else. There were a few of us living in that apartment, to keep the rent down. At the time, Callie was working at a sandwich shop and I was working at a school for kids who were in state custody. When I first started the job, I had to go to a special training on how to deal with the kids and how to restrain them when they got out of control. We spent the day doing take-downs and basket holds. There was a blackboard at the front of the room that said "danger = opportunity."

Callie's family lived far away and she never saw them. She had lots of brothers and sisters, and when she was little her father would take them to nude beaches and take movies of them, and then he'd sell the movies. There were other things that happened, too, things I don't want to mention here, things that aren't mine to mention. So now one of Callie's sisters didn't talk at all and the other one spoke in a funny voice and gave herself another name. Callie had some kind of uterine cancer that she was getting treated for, and her insides were all messed up. When I asked her about her family, she said -

"I miss my mother, but not my father, if you know what I mean."

"I know what you mean," I said.

Callie believed in divination, believed she could tell the future. She told me that I would do something good with my life, but couldn't tell me what, exactly. She told me I would help people, which was hard to believe then, when I couldn't even help myself. Callie said she practiced witchcraft, too - she had a little altar next to her bed with all kinds of symbols and rocks on it.

"I'm trying to cast a spell on you," she told me. "A love spell."

During the day, I went to my job, the one with the kids. After awhile my knees and elbows looked like bruised apples from all the restraints. I got promoted to the role of crisis counselor, which meant that I sat in a room with mats on the walls and waited for kids to be brought in, all riled up and ready to take somebody's head off. Or sometimes they'd call us over the intercom when a kid went crazy in a classroom and it was too dangerous to remove him.

"Support, Nancy needs help in Room 21," the intercom would say. They called us "support."

When the kids got angry they would try to make you angry, too, and they'd look for your weak spot, whatever it was that hurt you or made you ashamed or embarrassed. They'd accuse you of unseemly desires, or insult your ethnicity, or your religion – whatever would push the button. What I came to realize was that sometimes the kids *wanted* you to restrain them. They wanted you to bring them down and be on them like that, as close as could be, your body against theirs but still safe. They wanted you to save them from the acts of their darkest, most anguished selves. Over time, I came to see restraint for what it was: a gift of love.

At the end of every day, the buses would come. They lined up out front, and the intercom would tell us when to bring the kids down to the parking lot. The intercom would call each bus by number, and we came to remember which kid belonged on which bus. "*Laidlaw, 91664,*" the intercom would say, and I'd bring down Max and Travis, who'd destroyed all of the furniture in their classroom that day and broken a couch in half. Then the buses would take the children back to their group homes, where they did terrible things to one another when the staff wasn't watching.

There were some kids at the school who I still think about from time to time. There was a girl named Louanne who rocked and talked to herself all the time, and spoke of herself in the third person. She was taking some kind of medication - they all were, and it made them swell up like a bunch of baby cows. Louanne used to like to sit in my lap, and she'd tell me things in her strange, third-person way; never making eye contact, always talking to herself instead of the listener. There was a story about a bathtub, something that had happened in a bathtub, but that's all I could make out. Then I'd just let her sit there and I'd rock her.

Sometimes Louanne's father and mother would come

to visit her. A social worker would have to sit with them during the visit, because the father wasn't allowed to be alone with Louanne after the terrible things that he had done to her. Louanne and her family would have their visits in the schoolyard, at one of the picnic tables, and I could see them through the classroom window. Her father was short and squat and unkempt. Her mother had dark hair that hung like curtains around her face and was missing all of her front teeth. Louanne had a younger sister who would visit with them too, sometimes. The little girl still lived with the parents. She was pretty and smart and lucid, and she spoke in a regular voice. She had not been sacrificed.

After I'd been working at the school for awhile I started having dreams about the kids, and I had a dream about Louanne. I dreamt I met the real person, the person underneath. The person who would've been, who could've been. She was serene and thoughtful and soft-spoken. In the dream it was nighttime and we walked hand in hand through a dark forest. The night was peaceful and soft, and the road was made of sand. As we walked, we spoke in quiet voices about love, about what it is to love. We were not older and younger anymore, not teacher and student.

When I arrived in the classroom the next day, Louanne was sitting alone at her desk. She rocked quietly back and forth, and said my name.

Every day when I came home from work, Callie and I would walk outside, through the park, and Callie would take my arm and hold it. We talked about all kinds of things, anything we could think of. Sometimes I'd tell her about the kids at the school and all the crazy things they did. We talked about the suffering of those children, and the meaning of that suffering, or if there was one.

I told Callie about the squat albino boy who only spoke in hip-hop style rhyme, and the girl who thought she was a cat. I told her about another girl at the school named Myrna, who'd been kept in a dog kennel until she was four years old and child welfare finally came to rescue her. Myrna had short red hair and a sharp nose, and her blue eyes were piercing and intelligent. It was rumored that her grandmother was an Indian, and that her great-great grandparents had walked the Trail of Tears.

Most of the people at the school were afraid of Myrna, both teachers and students. She had kicked one teacher in the head and the woman developed seizures and sued the school. Another time she'd tried to choke someone with a scarf they were wearing. Myrna also liked to disrobe when the moment struck her, and she'd urinate and defecate in front of people. She did that sometimes when the nuns came around. It was a Catholic program, and every week or so the nuns came in and spoke to the kids. They'd stand at the front of the classroom, talking about nothing that meant anything to those kids at that moment, nothing that could help them just then, and Myrna would squat down alongside her desk and pee.

After awhile, I had a dream about Myrna, just like I'd had a dream about Louanne. I dreamt that we were on a bus trip together. We sat behind the bus driver, who had a thick scar around the circumference of his neck.

"He has the mark of the hanged man," Myrna said, "and because of that he has no peace."

After that, the bus driver, who saw everything there was to see, and knew everything there was to know, told us that the bombs had gone off and the world was coming to an end. He pulled over the bus and we dug trenches and lay down in them, and waited. We couldn't hear or see a thing, but we knew the end of the world was coming.

There were two of us crisis counselors at work, myself and a guy named Heshie. Heshie was short and muscular with long arms that dangled at his sides like an ape's. Sometimes Heshie would drive me home after work, and as time went on it took him longer and longer to stop talking and say goodbye. After awhile he started talking about relationships and that kind of thing, which was not a good sign. He would take my hand and hold it and not let it go, and I felt awkward and like I didn't know what to say or how to get my hand back. I wound up going out with Heshie a few times, and with other people, too, but it felt like just going through the motions, it felt like nothing. But sometimes you find yourself going along with things, you find yourself doing things that you don't really want to do, and later you wonder why you did them, and it just keeps on like that.

Sometimes Callie would wait up for me when I got home late, and I'd find her holding or hugging something of mine – a shirt or something – in the bed with her.

"Can't you see that Callie is in love with you?" One of our roommates said.

After awhile, Callie started collecting things of mine, little things, like a used tissue and some hair clippings she'd retrieved from the sink after I trimmed my hair.

"This isn't healthy," I said to her.

"Tell me about it," she said, but she couldn't help herself. She followed me on a couple of dates, and once she let the air out of somebody's tires. Sometimes she'd come into my room and cry, because she was losing herself in me, and I would cry too, because I was losing myself. We were like two people who'd jumped off a building together – entangled, struggling, plunging.

Eventually, Callie left town and moved to New York. I left shortly after that, and they threw a farewell party for me at the school, in the cafeteria. Heshie was the DJ, he set up the record player on one of the cafeteria tables and all the kids came down. Most of them had no idea what the party was for, but some of them did, and a few sat by me for the whole afternoon and held my hand or sat in my lap. Heshie played Michael Jackson songs and oldies like "Monster Mash" and "Kung-Fu Fighting." Some of the kids danced, and it was something to watch them. They gyrated and twirled, faces pointed toward the ceiling, oblivious to everything. Louanne spun in circles in a corner, alone. Her blue eyes were large and glassy, and she closed them from time to time as she moved. It was like a trance, like some kind of private prayer or ecstasy, as if she were hearing the word of God, and receiving it.

Like I said, Callie went to New York City, to be an artist. During the day she painted apartments with a group of Irish painters, and they would drink a lot while they worked. One day they were painting an apartment and Callie got so drunk that she passed out, and when she woke up she had no clothes on and the apartment was empty.

After that, Callie left that job, and she couldn't find another one. She couldn't pay for the room she was renting anymore and she started hanging out in Washington Square Park, with the homeless and the addicts, and she started using heroin. I went back to Oklahoma City, where I was from. I moved back with my parents, into the basement, while they sat upstairs in matching La-Z-Boy chairs, smoking themselves into oblivion. I kept on as I had been, til I didn't recognize myself, doing things and then wondering why I'd done them.

Callie never called me anymore. We didn't speak for a very long time. One day the police went to Washington Square Park and swept the area of vagrants, because they were lighting fires in trashcans and sleeping on benches. They took Callie, too – she was sleeping under a tree and hadn't showered in weeks. They had to chase her and she fought them like crazy, so by the time they got her into the paddy wagon she was completely naked, her clothes had been torn off in the struggle. They took her to Bellevue Hospital, and she stayed there for a long time.

It was after she got out that Callie called me. She said that she had a room now, in a boarding house, and a job at a flower shop. She told me that she'd gone to see a tea-leaf reader when she got out of the hospital, a Russian lady out on Coney Island. Callie said that she'd wanted to see the ocean when she got out – it was the first thing she wanted to do, the thing she'd dreamt about the whole time she was in there. But it turned out that Coney Island in the wintertime was gray and bleak, with car alarms going off and a decaying, decrepit kind of sadness.

Not a place where you'd expect to find a beach, Callie said, and I agreed.

Anyway, Callie had gone to have her tea leaves read, and the woman said that there was someone far away who wanted to see Callie, an old friend who needed her.

"Who are you to co-opt my tea leaf reading?" Callie said to me. But then she added - "The Russian lady said that you have to hold on. You have to wait."

It was sometime after that when Callie asked me to come to Fort Bloom to see her, and I went. When I met her at the boarding house her face was bright and there was something lifted, something dark that used to hover around her that was gone now. When we ate lunch together I kept looking at her arms, which had gouges and painful-looking craters in the crooks. We sat in the park and talked for a long time, and that night, when I slept over, she lay next to me breathing evenly until I fell asleep, and when I awoke I felt her cheek against mine.

"No one will know," she said, and I knew they wouldn't.

I never saw Callie again after that, but years later I heard that she had gotten sick. She'd gotten sick when she was living in the park and doing heroin, when she didn't care what happened to her and what people did to her, or what she did to herself. She'd gotten sick during the time when she let herself slip away, when she became lost from herself, and before she worked so hard to find herself again, like we both did—before we reeled ourselves in like kites struggling against the current of the wind.

Sometimes when I think about that time, I think about Callie, and the school, and the kids, and Louanne, and the dreams. Sometimes I wonder if Callie is still alive, and to tell you the truth, I don't think so. And then I think about that trip out into Brooklyn, how the train ride went on and on, and how empty the cars got; and how you didn't know where you were going and it made you feel scared inside, because you'd never been that way before. And I tell you, if you ever take a trip that far out into Brooklyn, it takes a very, very, long time.

Passengers

She loved the traveling, the in-betweens, which were always so much more satisfying than the arrival, the being there. Being there, being in a place, she felt lost; but traveling to the place was another thing altogether – like a synapse in which she felt whole and complete.

She was going to visit her daughter in another city. She did not go often enough, she and the daughter had been estranged. But things were improving now that the daughter had a child, now that the daughter saw the mother differently and there was a grandchild to fill the space between them.

The night before she departed, the woman had a dream, one she barely remembered. In it, she drove by a stand of trees—tall, stark pines like the kind she knew when she was a child in Southern Georgia. The trees were shrouded in hopelessness, but they were beautiful, somehow, too – straight and evenly spaced.

As she boarded the plane that morning she smiled at the stewardesses and the pilot who waited to greet her. The pilot's hair curled around his ears and his face was tan and smooth, but with deep creases down the sides so that he looked both young and old at the same time. She recalled reading somewhere that all airline pilots learned their trade in the military—the air force or navy, perhaps. She did not know if this was true, but she found it difficult to imagine this man as a soldier, with his soft face and gentle smile. The stewardesses were another story altogether: mostly blonde, darker toward the scalp, with sharp faces and severe make-up. They greeted her with a polite nod of acknowledgment. No one moved to help her with her carry-on.

The woman took her seat toward the middle of the plane and watched as the rest of the passengers boarded, thankful that her row had been called early. A handsome young man in a white shirt took the seat across the aisle from her, then struggled to fit his bag under the seat in front of him.

"That can fit overhead," she offered, helpfully.

He looked at her, startled, then shook his head.

"This is fine," he said, and sat back in his seat and faced front.

When he glanced at her again the woman smiled, because he looked a little bit nervous, and foreign, and she liked to smile at foreign-looking people right off, so they would know that she was friendly. He did not smile back, but sat very stiffly and straight.

"Nervous?" She smiled.

The young man barely glanced at her, kept his eyes on the seatback ahead of him. His hands were knotted in his lap.

Shortly after takeoff, the stewardesses began making their way down the aisle with drinks. The woman watched them, how they interacted with the passengers in a manner that was both solicitous and remote, and she imagined that they were trained to cultivate such a demeanor. She recalled reading, recently, about incidents in which drunken passengers had attacked flight attendants, over things like headsets and beer nuts. She imagined that after this the stewardesses were taught – Do not trust the passengers. They are full of need and want. They have secret, desperate pasts that might surface at any moment, in the full bloom of violence. Keep them at arm's length, serve them, but offer nothing of yourselves.

When it was her turn to receive a beverage, the woman asked for a tomato juice. As expected, the stewardess gave her a half-smile but kept her face stern. The young man across from her ordered nothing. Occasionally, his eyes would dart to the left or right or to his feet. She imagined that this must be his first time flying, and she was tempted to try and comfort him again. She looked at him sidelong to determine if he might be more receptive now to her efforts. She could see now how lovely he was, with dark hair that fell in bangs across his forehead, and a face that still had a soft, adolescent look, almost feminine. It was a beauty that belonged to young men for only a short time, she thought; before their faces and bodies filled out and became coarse, before the look of gentle vulnerability disappeared and they became hard and ordinary.

The woman thought flickeringly of her own son, Herbie. Herbie had played football when he was in high school. She still kept a picture of him in his uniform - kneeling with his hand on his helmet, lanky and angular and with too many teeth. He'd been found dead in somebody's basement a year ago, wrapped in an old carpet. His face and hands were blue. She had not known that he'd been using heroin.

Impulsively, she reached out and touched the sleeve of the young man who sat across the aisle from her.

"Don't be afraid," she said.

When the drinks were finished, people began settling in for the flight – shoes came off, books and magazines came out. People cozied up against the windows and lowered the shades halfway, to shield against the oncoming sun. The woman leaned her head back against the seat and closed her eyes, and felt how tired she was, even in the early morning. It was a deep tired that never really left her no matter how much she slept, and in a few moments it pulled her down into a kind of trance, into that crazy area between sleeping and waking, where thoughts and images collide nonsensically. She saw Herbie there, as always. He was sitting upright, in a brightly lit room. He was wearing the robe that she had bought him, open at the neck and chest. He was smiling at her serenely, peacefully, but there was something about the image that made her uneasy, and she felt herself pulling away from it, as she often did. From there she drifted into a dream about two rocks separating, disclosing a small tree. There was something about butterflies, too, or feathers, she wasn't sure which. It was pleasant, and she found herself wanting to linger there, until from a great distance she heard someone calling her. She tried to resist it, but it continued, and after awhile she felt herself being pulled down the long corridor toward wakefulness.

As the sound persisted, the woman had an increasing sense that someone needed her, that it was important that she awaken quickly, but her body fought her, exhausted. It was like being deep underwater and swimming slowly toward the surface, the sun frighteningly far away. But she willed herself up through the layers of her sleep, not knowing quite why, and emerged like a diver up through the waves – all at once and sputtering.

When she opened her eyes she saw her young man – he was standing in the aisle and shouting. At first she thought that there must be something wrong with him, that he needed help, because it seemed so unlike him to draw attention to himself in this way. But then she realized that there were other voices, too, and when she looked around she saw other people standing, also shouting. She felt confused and foggy, groping, like there was something happening around her that she was supposed to understand but couldn't. Her young man and some other men began moving up the aisle, toward the front of the plane, still shouting. She wondered what they had done wrong, the passengers; how they had managed to arouse such anger. Then her young man turned back and she saw that he had something in his hand, and he continued to jab at the air with it, and she saw his face. Thoughts kept darting through her mind and she couldn't seem to hold onto any one of them, they were like slippery fish. But as the men moved closer to the cockpit she suddenly understood, and she felt herself bolt up sharply, and grab the back of the seat in front of her.

On the ground below, a woman stepped out of a small farmhouse and looked at the day around her. It was early morning but the sky was already a rare, brilliant blue, a day that must be used to its utmost, she thought. In the distance she could see the cornfields, and her husband, a small speck on a tractor. The machinery moved slowly, tilling under the unpicked ears. She smiled and headed toward the garden, where she would pick some of the last vegetables that the season would offer.

Once there, the woman knelt in the dirt and began to fill her basket, and let herself think for awhile about nothing in particular. As she worked, she sang softly to herself, until after awhile she noticed a faint accompaniment, a distant hum that seemed to grow louder with each passing moment until it overpowered the sound of her voice. She looked up then, at what she knew was a passing airplane. The plane was flying too low, she thought, and seemed to slow and then speed up, to wend its way across the sky uncertainly. She sat back on her heels and watched the plane as it passed over the cornfield, and traveled far over the neighboring farms. It seemed to straighten out a bit then, and to veer about slowly, like an elbow, until it had taken on a new direction altogether. She looked out toward the cornfield and saw that her husband had stopped the tractor and was watching the plane as well. His eyes followed the object until it disappeared from view, no part of him moving until the faint sound of the jet engine had faded entirely, and the day and sky were left just the same as they had been before. Then she heard her husband start the tractor again, and heard it rumble into motion.

She continued to sit on her haunches for a few moments, looking out in the direction where the plane had gone. She sat like that for awhile and noticed again the brilliant, stark blueness of the sky. She closed her eyes and felt the faint breeze stir her hair, and tried to will herself to think again about nothing in particular. She tried to think only about the coming of the fall, and how quickly the weather would change, and how grateful she should be for such a day, which was surely one of the last of its kind.

Some of the men made their way up to the front of the airplane. Others stayed back with the passengers, including the young man, who continued shouting and making nervous gestures with the object he held in his hands. His face was sweating. The stewardess tried to calm the passengers, tried to remember all she had been taught about such circumstances. She wondered where the men were taking them, whether they would want ransom, how long it would go on. It was all unknowable. She no longer wore an expression of aloofness, of course. She was frightened, and all of her humanity had rushed to the surface and showed on her face, the things she loved were in her face, the things she was afraid to lose.

From where she stood, the stewardess could hear commotion in the cockpit now, some scuffling and a muffled scream. She spied a pot of coffee on a burner, and she reached for it without thinking, a weapon. But before she stepped forward, before she sacrificed herself, she had a flickering, tragic recollection. She thought of the time, years ago, when she was going through the part of her training that dealt with crises – emergency landings, loss of pressure, cabin fires. They had practiced using the slides, the rafts, the oxygen, the exits; the things they would need in the event that they were going to die. And she remembered, during that part of the training, wondering if a day like this would ever come, if she would ever be called upon to use those special skills, the knowledge that no one could see or guess beneath the surface. Perhaps somewhere inside her, in the most secret of places, she had wondered if one day she would be called upon to do more than organize, arrange, and serve. And maybe, she thought with anguish, in some part of herself a long time ago, she had momentarily dreamt that such a moment would come; that it would save her soul from obscurity and bring about the emergence of her true self, and that her life would thereby be made exceptional.

In the back of the airplane, the woman leaned back in her seat, drained. The new pilots had taken the plane upwards, rapidly, and then plunged it downward at an abrupt angle. Now they were moving forward at a high rate of speed, accelerating with each passing second, and the plane shifted to the left and right erratically. Several of the passengers were vomiting and others were crying, wailing. A stewardess lay in the aisle, bleeding from the neck and chest.

The woman clutched the yellow vomit bag in her lap. She thought about using the Airphone, like some of the other passengers were doing, but she couldn't think of what she would say or who she would call. She thought for a moment about calling her daughter to tell her not to pick her up at the airport, but her hands wouldn't work to grasp the receiver. She imagined the baby crying in her car seat, and her daughter growing angry as she waited, looking at her watch. The woman looked out the window and could see a blur of buildings and a city below. She had lost her bearings, and was not entirely sure which city it was, but there was something about it that was familiar. They were flying low now, just above the skyline.

In the distance, she could see a large, dark structure approaching. She watched it, listless and ill. As they grew closer she began to recognize the building, and its double. The plane was moving even faster now, and the phantom grew larger, closer, until it dominated their field of vision and its image filled every portal. All the passengers were wailing and crying out in unison now, in a moment of sudden comprehension and anguish. Now they saw and understood everything.

The structure continued to grow and they hurtled toward it, a large, black force that loomed before them. It was all that could be seen now, and all there was - the massive, unknowable face of the building, terrible and unspeakable and profane.

It was all around them now, the woman thought; commanding them like destiny, drawing them into itself like a dark and unfathomable God, and she felt herself kneel down.

Acknowledgments

With deepest thanks to all who helped and encouraged in the publication of this book. With gratitude to the writer whose name I do not know, whose work helped to inspire the story *The Deepest, Darkest Part Of The Woods*.